Michael Hardcastle was born in Huddersfield in Yorkshire. After leaving school he served in the Royal Army Educational Corps before embarking on a career in journalism, working in a number of roles for provincial daily newspapers from reporter to chief feature writer.

He has written more than one hundred children's books since his first was published in 1966, but still finds time to visit schools and colleges all over Britain to talk about books and writing. In 1988 he was awarded an MBE in recognition of his services to children's books. He is married and lives in Beverley, Yorkshire.

D0726814

Eye for a Goal

Michael Hardcastle

Goal Kings
BOOK TWO

faber and faber
LONDON · BOSTON

First published in 1998
by Faber and Faber Limited
3 Queen Square London WC1N 3AU

Typeset by Avon Dataset, Bidford-on-Avon, Warwickshire
Printed and bound in England by Mackays of Chatham PLC,
Chatham, Kent

Michael Hardcastle is hereby identified as author of this work in
accordance with Section 77 of the Copyright, Designs and
Patents Act 1988

A CIP record for this book
is available from the British Library

ISBN 0-571-19143-6

2 4 6 8 10 9 7 5 3 1

Contents

1 Injury Time

'Ow!' came a loud cry from the junk cupboard. 'Ow, ow!'

'Josh, what's wrong?' his mother called. 'What've you done?' Grabbing a towel to dry her hands, she rushed from the kitchen to the walk-in cupboard opposite the front door.

Josh was gingerly backing out, his hands clasped to his forehead. Karen Rowley could just see the tears between his fingers.

'Stupid, stupid tennis!' he was muttering fiercely. 'Shouldn't even be there. Poking out like that – nearly poked my eye out!'

His mother gently prised his hands apart and examined his face for damage. There was a red mark, just above his right eye, possibly a scratch as well.

'No real damage done,' she said cheerfully. 'You'll live, Josh. No need to get upset like this.'

'But if I'd hurt my eye I wouldn't be able to play football and that would be the end of the world,' he declared, his lower lip still quivering.

'Nonsense!' said his mother. 'Come and have some milk. That'll help you calm down. And I can have a better look at your face in the light.'

Reluctantly, Josh followed her back to the kitchen, working out an answer to the question she was bound to ask. He kept the milk in his mouth as long as possible, just letting it dribble down his throat when she wanted to know why he wasn't wearing his glasses.

'It was too dark to see, anyway, so I was just using my hands to find the ball,' he replied slowly.

'Your glasses are there to help you whether it's dark or bright,' she pointed out. 'Josh, you've got to get used to them, *got* to. If you don't then you'll have a serious accident one day and Mr Saxton won't have you in his team then, will he? Not if you've really injured yourself.'

'Probably won't have me in the team whatever I do if I'm in glasses,' Josh said despairingly. 'Sam the Slammer doesn't rate me even though I do better tricks on the ball than anyone else in the Kings. Well, almost anyone.'

Mrs Rowley decided to change the subject. 'Why's he called Sam the Slammer? Very odd name.'

'Don't know. Don't care. Because he's a hard man, I suppose. Everybody calls him that. He knows it's his name and he seems to like it.'

His mother nodded as if it was what she expected to be told. She moved on to something else. 'What were you after in the junk cupboard, anyway?'

Josh said, 'My football, of course. I'd've found it easily if that stupid tennis racket hadn't hit me over the eye. Shouldn't be there!'

'Well, you see, it should. Now the tennis season's over Chrissie has got to put it somewhere for the winter. It's where we keep sports equipment – you know that better than anyone.' She paused and then added, 'I suppose part of the problem is that you're getting so tall, just shooting up and up. A few weeks ago that racket wouldn't have been low enough to poke you in the eye, or the forehead.'

Josh didn't say anything but secretly he was pleased with his new height. It already helped at football and he was sure things would get better still.

'Feeling better now?' his mother enquired, returning from the junk cupboard.

'Yes,' he admitted.

'Good,' she said, handing him the football and his spectacles. 'Now, be sensible and put them ON. You've got to accept they're necessary. That's a fact of life, like my chubby cheeks, Chrissie's blonde hair and your dad's, er, long legs. Things that can't be changed.'

Josh nodded, seeing nothing to be gained by discussing the matter further. He bounced the ball out of the house and into the back garden where he practised volleying it against the blank wall of next door's garage and plotted how to convince Sam that he should be picked as a striker for the Goal Kings' next match against Stonecreek Pirates.

'Was it a good goal that you scored, then?'

Sam wanted to know when he saw Josh.

'Sorry?' Josh was completely baffled by the question.

'The goal, son, the one you must have scored with your nut. Had to, to get that scratchy mark on your forehead. Or did their goalie connect with his fist?'

Josh tried to work out a satisfactory answer. Sam didn't like to be told he was wrong about anything. 'It wasn't like that, Boss,' he said cautiously, careful to use a form of address Sam liked. 'I just barged into something, that's all.'

'You weren't wearing your glasses, then? Given them up, have you?'

'The man said they weren't always necessary,' was the calculated reply. Josh could only pray that Sam wouldn't enquire about the man's identity. With luck the coach would assume it was an optician.

'Oh, I see – sorry, no pun intended!' Clearly it was intended, so Josh shared in the laughter. 'As you keep growing up, you'll grow out of your eye problem. Is that it?'

'I suppose that must be it,' Josh agreed thankfully.

'Or are you wearing contact lenses now?' the coach suddenly shot at him. 'They can be a problem in themselves, you know.'

'Definitely not,' Josh assured him with a smile to indicate that, really, everything was fine. To his relief, other members of the Kings' squad arrived and began to kick a ball around as they awaited Sam's instructions. First, though, Sam had something else to say to Josh.

'I'm giving you a marking job today,' he said. 'I want to see if you can stick like glue to an opponent, make sure he never gets in a kick or a header.'

'But I'm a striker,' Josh protested. 'You know –'

'*You* know, Josh, that I switch people around all the time. That way, nobody gets complacent. Everybody gets a chance to show what they can do. And I find out who is best in every position.'

Josh hadn't really been listening to that revealing disclosure of Sam Saxton's style of management. All he could think about was how it applied to him.

'Why me?' he asked anxiously. 'Why can't

someone else do a marking job? I'm best at scoring goals. You know that, Boss. So just let me score some more today.'

Alex Todd laughed. 'You haven't scored a real goal for years. Tap-ins, that's you, Josh, tap-ins. So –'

'That's not true!' Josh, face reddening, turned on the team's star player, himself a talented striker. 'I hit one in from, from twenty metres against Silverton.'

Alex laughed again, louder. 'Yeah, that was a great strike. The ball bounced four times before it reached the net and nobody was there to stop it because the goalie was crawling around on his hands and knees at the edge of the box after Foggy had knocked him over. It amazed me the ref didn't blow up for a foul. He must have been unsighted. So that's why your terrific goal was allowed.'

Josh swallowed. His arguing was finished. Alex's description couldn't be faulted. All he could add was that at least his aim had been good because the ball went arrow-straight into the net. But that wasn't worth pointing out.

Foggy was bounding up to them. 'Hey, I'm

a striker! I'm a striker!' he announced, thunderously. 'I'm going to take you on, Josh. So get ready for a rough time, a really rough time.'

Josh blinked. He knew he blinked a lot and wished he didn't. People suspected it was caused by an eye problem but Josh didn't believe that: he simply blinked if something surprised him. That was perfectly normal. Everybody did it.

'When I show 'em how good I am in the air old Sam will pick me to lead the attack all the time, no danger,' Foggy went on in the voice that resembled the foghorn from which his nickname was derived. 'Even you, Alex, had better watch out. I mean, the selectors will see *me* and no one else will matter after that.'

'Right,' declared Sam, having heard none of that. 'Let's practise a few set pieces. We're not scoring enough goals from corners and free kicks. We've got to do better, be better organized, be *prepared*. Make certain *we* get the ball, *we* create the chances.'

Tugging firmly at his favourite baseball cap, he set up a corner situation first, instruc-

8

ting Matthew to send over a variety of crosses, just making sure the ball was really airborne. 'Nothing on the ground this time, we want to see how good players are in the *air*.' Somehow he managed to look at Josh and Foggy simultaneously, so they had no doubt who he meant.

Foggy wasn't tall, he was stocky, but he could jump well, just as he could do many things well that required athleticism. He soared as the ball came across but to his amazement Josh reached it first, nodding it quite gently away from his opponent. Foggy, coming down to earth, glared at him.

'How d'you do that?' he demanded. 'You can't outjump me.'

'I just did,' replied Josh, surprised as well as pleased by his success. He hadn't imagined it would be so simple to get to the ball ahead of a boy who often seemed so good at everything.

'You won't do it again!' said Foggy fiercely. Yet for once his voice was almost quiet.

Josh had expected some reaction, praise even, from Sam. But the Slammer said nothing at all. Perhaps he didn't see what I did,

Josh told himself. So he'd have to repeat it, keeping his fingers crossed it would work perfectly again. This time, though, he'd try to head the ball harder.

They had to wait for some time before the corner kick came across to them. Josh and Foggy rose together but Josh was soon falling back, clutching hard at the place where Foggy's elbow had been driven like a dagger into his ribs. The pain was intense. He didn't even see Foggy divert the ball into the net, winning a 'Well done!' from Sam.

'Why did you do that?' Josh gasped when he could speak, though he knew the answer.

'You were getting in my way. I don't let that happen to me. I'm a winner, I've always got to win.'

'But I'm a team-mate,' Josh pointed out.

'Not when we're on opposite sides, like now,' Foggy said. 'I'd kick my old grannie over the moon if she got in my way. Getting the ball first, that's what this game's all about.'

Josh didn't say anything, simply made up his mind what he must do. There was an interval before the ball came floating towards them again. Foggy, impatient as usual, rose a fraction too soon. Josh, timing his jump better, got to the ball easily. But, just to make sure Foggy couldn't outwit him in any way, his hands went down on Foggy's neck. He pushed strongly. Foggy, thoroughly surprised, stumbled so badly as he landed he finished up in a heap. Josh laughed, laughed at the ease of his success and the sight of Foggy helpless.

'Glad to hear you're enjoying yourself,' boomed Sam, timing his viewing perfectly. 'You did well there, Josh, showed proper aerial power *and* determination. Hope it wasn't a fluke.'

It wasn't clear to Josh whether Sam had seen the push but even if he had he plainly didn't disapprove. The reverse, really. 'Thanks, Boss,' he said politely. He glanced at Foggy but the boy with the voice was mute. Then, to Josh's amazement, Foggy winked at him. Just what he meant by that gesture Josh didn't know but he felt sure Foggy would treat him differently in future: for Josh had shown unquestionably that he wasn't a pushover.

'Boss!' Josh called as he saw Sam turn away to run his eye over a group keenly involved in a tackling exercise. 'Boss, will I be in the team for the game against the Pirates?'

Sam raised his eyebrows. 'Could be, Josh, could be,' he responded in a thoughtful tone. 'You seem to be doing all right since you left your specs off. No problem there now, is there?'

It was a comment rather than a question but Josh felt compelled to answer. 'No, no, I'm fine,' he said quickly. 'Can see everything I need to.' In terms of accuracy, it was a long way from the truth but Josh forced himself not to think about that at this time of high success in the eyes of Sam the Slammer.

During the previous season he'd been left out of the side more often than he'd played; and even when he was picked it was usually in defence. Yet Josh believed he was a natural attacker because he had pace, positional sense and plenty of courage (well, he was *convinced* he would display all the bravery necessary to win something for his beloved Kings but to date he hadn't been called upon to perform any real heroics). Now he might get his chance.

'Right, we'll just have one more go, see if we can learn anything useful for the game against the Pirates,' Sam said as he organized a new defensive wall that was practically crescent-shaped. 'Josh, you get into this central position. Your height should be the best barrier of the lot. So don't lose sight of the ball whatever you do.'

'Right, Boss,' Josh replied eagerly, tugging at his shorts to give his hands something to do while waiting for the kick to be taken. It was a long time since Sam Saxton had paid him so much attention. That *must* mean he was going to be chosen for Sunday's game. Desperate though he was to be a striker, he knew he'd be perfectly willing to play any-where.

The Kings' coach signalled to Matthew Forrest to swing in a cross at the required height. Matthew, popularly known among the squad as Tree, was a newcomer to Rodale and so far hadn't established a place in the team. Although he could hit a ball accurately a long way he didn't seem to have many other qualities as a player. To Sam, however, he was something of a challenge because there must be room for improvement in the burly, dark-haired Welsh boy.

As the ball flew towards the wall it suddenly swerved and dipped as if it had been fired in by a cricketer's spinning fingers. Josh, just taking off, had to change direction, too. He hurled himself headlong at the ball before it could hit the ground and unluckily met Alex's rising boot as the striker jumped and stretched in a valiant bid to volley the ball over wall and keeper and into the net.

Josh collapsed to the ground, clutching his left cheek with both hands and uttering not a sound. Sam turned and called to Davey Stroud who was standing nearest the touchline, 'Grab my medical bag and bring it over here quick!' Then he dashed across to Josh, still lying prone. 'Come on, son, let me see what's wrong. I'm sure you'll be fine in a minute.'

Reluctantly, Josh took one of his hands away so that the affected area could be examined. It hurt badly, far worse than when he'd bumped into the protruding tennis racket at home. If he'd broken something then he wouldn't be playing again for a long time.

That was the thought in his mind in spite of the pain.

'I'm putting on something that'll really help,' Sam told him soothingly. 'It'll be freezing but don't worry, it'll do a lot of good. Just hold it against your cheek – that's right.'

'Ow!' Josh jumped. He couldn't help it. The bag of ice that had been in the cool-box all evening took his breath away. Now the pain seemed to be spreading all through his head.

'You're going to be fine, Josh,' the coach tried to reassure him. 'The damage should be no more than bruising. I'd've known if it'd been worse. Good job it was a boot and not a brick in your face! And you were brave to go for the ball, Josh. I admire that, son.'

The pain was receding and the praise helped to send it on its way. Carefully, Josh sat up, opening his eyes to see several curious faces peering at him. Alex was holding out his hand and saying, 'Sorry, Josh. Just an accident, honest. I don't go around kicking my mates!'

'Just kicks opponents, that's all!' Foggy boomed and everyone laughed. Even Josh managed a twisted grin.

'That's better, Josh,' Sam declared, and there was a note of relief in his voice. 'Keep that ice-pack on a bit longer and it'll prevent any swelling. Probably all you'll be left with is a bruise. With that one on your forehead you're obviously starting a collection.'

Josh tried to put out of his mind what his health-conscious mum might say. There was bound to be an inquest into his use, or rather non-use, of his glasses in spite of the fact that it would have been a good deal worse had he been wearing them when he was kicked. *Terrible* that would have been. He shuddered.

A few minutes later, following an exercise designed to sharpen everyone's skills when running with the ball and trying to outwit an opponent, Sam announced that they'd done enough for one night. It was time to pack up and go home and dream of glory, as he put it, entirely accurately. There wasn't a single player in the Kings' squad who didn't daydream about hitting unstoppable shots to win Cup Finals and collect man-of-the-match medals. And that included even devoted defenders who scarcely crossed the half-way line in any game!

'So, how're you feeling now, Josh?' he enquired sympathetically as they walked towards the changing rooms on the far side of the all-weather pitch.

'Oh, great, thanks, Boss!' Josh replied eagerly, though in truth his cheek was throbbing and there was a dull ache somewhere in his midriff, probably a legacy of Foggy's elbowing. 'Er, do you think I played well tonight? I mean, you said I was brave to go for that ball with a diving header.'

'I did, and I meant it. But that doesn't mean you're definitely in the team for the Stonecreek match, Josh,' the coach replied deflatingly. 'Oh yes, I know that's what you're thinking about. But I've got to be sure about everyone before I pick a team. So let's just say you're among the possibles.'

Alex, who'd been listening to the conversation, had his own question for Sam Saxton. 'Are you definitely playing for United Exes tomorrow night, Mr Saxton?' he enquired in a neutral tone.

Sam shot him a sharp glance. 'Well, I'm hoping so. Depends on who turns up, really. Could be a lot of competition. Anyway, how d'you know about this game, Alex?'

'Saw a poster on the noticeboard at the leisure centre. Listed some of the ex-players who might be turning out. Your name's there. Oh yes, and my dad mentioned it, too. Said United are hoping to raise loads and loads of money for Jeff's testimonial fund. I mean, that was a terrible injury he got, wasn't it? Must be the worst feeling in the world to know you can *never* ever play football again.'

Sam looked at Alex, more calculatingly this time, but didn't speak. His mind was wrestling with several thoughts. Matthew Forrest, who'd overheard Alex's remarks, had a question for him.

'Who is this Jeff and what happened to him?'

'United's star striker a few years ago. Dad's always going on about him because he was so good. Had just picked up his first England cap when he broke a leg. Terrible accident in the goalmouth, Dad said. It put him out of the game and this testimonial match is to help raise money for him, for his future. I think he was only about twenty when it happened. Is that right, Mr Saxton?'

'More or less,' Sam nodded. 'As you're displaying such a keen interest in this match are you planning to be there, Alex?'

'No way! Danny and I are getting some badminton practice in.' He looked round in conspiratorial fashion in case the person he was about to mention might be within ear-shot. 'We want to improve so that we can surprise Foggy when we take him on next time.'

'Oh, I see.' It was news to Sam that the Kings' most effective striker (when he was on form and not sulking) and their goal-keeper, Danny Loxham, had become playing partners. But he could understand their determination not to be Foggy's victims.

'But I think Dad's going to the game,' Alex added unexpectedly. 'He said last night he'd never actually seen you in action for United. Not in a competitive game, anyway. So this is his chance. Oh, and he said it was all in a good cause, anyway, so he won't mind putting his hand in his pocket.'

Sam suspected there might be another motive for making those comments but he wasn't going to risk saying anything. If Ricky

Todd turned up at the match then he'd be sure to say something about it the next time he met Sam.

'Hey, I didn't know you used to play for United!' exclaimed Matthew Forrest, who'd just been given the news in a whisper from Josh. 'Were you a big star player? Did you have kids queuing up for your autograph?'

'No, I didn't, and that's enough about the past,' Sam replied sharply. 'All we should be talking about, thinking about, is the future. The future of Rodale Goal Kings. Nothing is as important as that.'

'Just what my dad says,' said Alex Todd, who always liked to have the last word on any subject.

2 Past and Future Glories

In spite of lightly falling rain and a distant chill in the air, a sizeable crowd had turned up at the Town Ground to pay tribute to Jeff Starkie, the former United star who had so cruelly been put out of the game. Several of his former team-mates were in the present United side which was playing a team billed as 'United's Golden Exes', a name that amused some and annoyed others.

'Better than Golden Oldies, though, isn't it?' joked Billy Coltman to Sam Saxton as they lined up together to be introduced to the crowd by a well-known radio disc jockey who'd been handed the public address microphone for the occasion. 'Personally, I don't think I even qualified for the silver section!'

Sam smiled but didn't say anything. If Billy, who went on to captain a First Division side, felt that then Sam himself was lucky to get any invitation at all. For in his career he'd played only a score of games for United's first team. Still, it was nice to be remembered and so he hadn't wanted to miss the game in spite of his wife's doubts about playing in a competitive match at his age. Moreover, he enjoyed wearing again the famous old black and white stripes and feeling an integral part of a team. He'd heard many former players complain that they'd given up the game too soon because there was never any real substitute for playing; and Sam had come round to that view, too.

Spectators were still trickling into the ground as the match kicked off and it looked as though Jeff Starkie was going to finish up with a handsome pay-out. Although he'd come out into the middle to meet the players who were raising money for him and tossed-up, his injury didn't allow him to perform the one thing he'd've loved: actually kicking the ball into play. Sam looked at Jeff, years younger than himself, and thought about the pain he must have endured behind the smile he was putting on for the public's benefit.

United, fielding two or three of their current stars but mostly represented by second-team players, swept upfield immediately and so put the Exes under what all commentators and papers describe as pressure. Sam didn't manage a touch for the first couple of minutes even though the ball bobbed around the goalmouth until Billy Coltman hoofed it clear. Already it was plain that this wouldn't be any form of exhibition match: United were playing to win because so many of the team wanted recognition and a place of their own in the senior side.

Sam's first contribution was a firm header when he got to the ball a micro-second ahead of United's tigerish striker; and it pleased him because he'd got both his timing and the direction right. Having not played at this level for a very long time he'd worried that he might be completely out of touch. A 'friendly' game it might be, but he couldn't afford to look a fool in front of a lot of people who knew him personally. Among the crowd would be parents of Kings' players and perhaps some of the boys themselves. So for his own self-respect he needed to acquit himself well throughout the game.

After five minutes United took the lead through their thrusting young striker McCool. Bursting into the box to reach a raking cross from his winger, he brushed aside Sam's challenge and, pouncing on the ball, hit it first time into the far top corner of the net. By most standards it was an excellent and spectacular goal, just the sort of thing the crowd had paid to see. Almost everyone enjoyed it.

Sam didn't. He really should have prevented that goal, he should have taken the ball off McCool's toes before he had a chance to strike. He'd been a fraction slow to react to the cross and the penalty was severe. Sam set high standards for himself as well as for his young players. So he was thoroughly annoyed with himself. Next time he mustn't make a mistake.

Next time came sooner than he'd expected. Once again McCool was the prime attacker and now was swapping one-twos with a partner. Sam carefully backed off, waiting for the moment to tackle and win the ball. McCool casually turned one way and then, with vivid acceleration, darted in the opposite direction. Sam, half-leaning the wrong way, twisted sharply to correct his position – and collapsed.

The pain was awful. His knee, his leg, was on fire. He had to bite his lower lip to prevent himself from crying out. He knew immediately he wouldn't play a game of football again for a very long time.

As he waited for the stretcher that would be needed Sam berated himself for his folly in turning out in a game like this when he wasn't really fit enough: well, not fit enough to cope with the speed of players of McCool's standard. All he could hope was that he hadn't done irreparable harm that could prevent him ever walking again. The first diagnosis by a physio present at the Town Ground wasn't encouraging, and so his fears grew as a car rushed him to hospital. There a thorough investigation disclosed torn ligaments. Recovery was going to take some time and surgery might be necessary. Meanwhile, Sam was strapped up, provided with painkillers and sent home, there to rest as much as possible and keep his leg in an elevated position.

'I feel dreadful,' he told his wife Marina as she drove him back to Rodale after being summoned from the home of a friend she'd been visiting that evening. 'And please, *please*, don't say to me "I told you so, Sam!" That's no help now it's happened.'

'But I *did*,' she couldn't help saying. 'I warned you it was time you packed it all in and just settled for happy memories of past glories. The body doesn't last for ever, you know.'

'Bit macabre, that,' he said, frowning. 'I mean, I've only damaged a knee, it's not life-threatening! I'll soon be back to normal, you'll see.'

'But normal doesn't include kicking a football around, or showing other people how to do it. The hospital says an injury like yours is a shock to the system, so you've got to make sure there's no repetition. So coaching is OUT, understand?'

'But – but –'

'No buts, thank you,' she cut in. 'Your boys' team is going to have to find somebody else to look after them. Anyway, it just wouldn't look good, would it, you trying to coach young players while on crutches?'

He couldn't really disagree with that view-point. In any case, he was feeling much too uncomfortable to indulge in an argument. After being always so active he guessed it would take him a long time to adjust to life on crutches.

It took no time at all for word to get round the village of Rodale Kings that Sam Saxton had been carried off in a testimonial match and, like the ex-player he'd been helping to raise money for, might never kick a football again. Even before he and Marina got home from hospital their phone was ringing with messages of sympathy and, in the case of one caller, an enquiry about who might take over the running of the Sunday Junior League side.

Because he tended to run things entirely in his own way, and not rely on anybody else for support in any respect, Sam wasn't pop-ular with everyone who had something to do with Rodale Goal Kings. Several parents rather resented his refusal ever to discuss team selections with them or admit them to changing-rooms before or after a match. Parents or supporters who wanted to play a larger part in, say, fund-raising activities or presentation nights were often discouraged by Sam's regular comment, 'Oh, I've got all that in hand. Best just leave such matters to me.' He didn't even like to discuss tactics or future plans with anyone. One or two parents who had very positive ideas about changes in style of play or different formations had been politely listened to; and that was as far as Sam took things.

Still, it was hard to argue against his control because he'd guided the Kings to a notable triumph the previous season: they'd won the Highlea Sunday League Knock-out Cup in a memorable final decided by a penalty shoot-out. True, their record in the League had not been so impressive and, at the half-way stage of the season, there'd been real fears among some supporters that the team would be relegated. However, victory in the Cup Final, played early in the New Year, seemed to have stimulated the players to such an extent that they'd finished the season comfortably in mid-table. Sam had declared at the concluding presentation night that 'the Goal Kings will build on the success of the Cup Final and really battle for the Championship next season.'

Now, though, with the new season barely launched it was clearly going to be difficult for Sam to keep his promise to drive or at least lead them to new honours in the months ahead. Ricky Todd, who heard the news of the injury from a friend who was an avid United fan and therefore never missed one of their matches, knew this was his moment to take over. He would never have a better chance to put into practice all the ideas he had for turning the Goal Kings into true champions, a team that would not only live up to their name but establish a reputation for excellence that would extend far, far beyond the county's boundaries. Ricky wanted them to have their own identifiable spot on the national map. So he wasted no time at all in ringing round as many players' families as possible to win over their support for his case to be sworn in as the Kings' new coach.

It was typical of his forward thinking that

he contacted first those parents he suspected might be his rivals for the job if, that is, they wanted it: Steve Parbold and Clark Kelly. If he could make sure they were out of the running then there shouldn't be any opposition for him to worry about because he was pretty sure the team's supporters wouldn't want to bring in an outsider.

Steve, father of Joe, the Kings' captain and rock-solid central defender, seemed quite amazed when Ricky asked if he were at all interested in taking on the role. 'Don't think I'm qualified, mate,' he replied at once. 'Have quite a bit of trouble keeping myself fit so I don't see how I could be responsible for the fitness of a horde of starving boys. Also, I like my evenings and Sundays free when I can get 'em. I'm a bit of a fanatic about model railways, you see, and there's always improvements to make in the layout and rolling stock, that sort of thing. Anyway, I'm sure you'd do a better job yourself, Ricky. I mean, you're the keen one, really keen, aren't you?'

Relieved, Ricky agreed, and salted away Steve's promise of support if the matter came to a vote. He doubted, though, whether Clark would surrender so easily and he was right. His son, Kieren, was an inconsistent but ambitious player, a defender who occasionally made horrendous mistakes on the ball. However, his parents, Clark and Jakki, had begun to take an increasingly active role as team supporters and thus appeared – to Ricky, anyway – to have won over Sam to their belief that Kieren should always be in the side.

'It's a bit early to be thinking of replacing Sam, isn't it?' Clark said as soon as he worked out the purpose of Ricky's call. 'He might be able to carry on perfectly well after a little rest.'

'I doubt that. I've already spoken to his wife and she says if she gets her way Sam will give up football altogether. I'm afraid Sam's injury is pretty bad, Clark.' Only some of that was true: so far no one had made any genuine medical forecasts about Sam's future fitness. But Ricky was confident Clark wouldn't know that.

'Well, I don't see there's any real *urgency* about making changes,' Clark replied. 'I mean, the team's in good shape and –'

'But there are *vital* matches coming up,' Ricky bulldozered through. 'First there's this League game against Stonecreek. *Very* tough opposition. Then we start the defence of the Knock-out Cup. Clark, if we don't get off to a cracking start we could struggle for the rest of the season. Believe me, there's got to be a firm hand at the helm.'

Clark's mind had been on another matter. 'You wanted to take over the team last season, didn't you? Just around New Year, time of the Cup Final.'

'I was ready to step in and *help*,' Ricky said smoothly and far from truthfully. 'If you remember, we were going through a bad time in the League. At that point we didn't know we were going to win the Cup, which then gave our League form a boost. Clark, all I'm concerned about is the success of the team, not personal glory. I'm just pleased to be a member of the *back-up* team, the fellas who help to keep the show on the road. Like yourself, of course.'

'I don't do much, do I?' Clark said, though it wasn't really a question. He hadn't wanted this conversation in the first place and was keen to get out of it in the face of Ricky's determination to get his own way. 'Jakki does more than I do. Fact is, she's got quite interested in the game.'

'So you don't fancy becoming coach yourself, then, when Sam, er, steps aside?'

'No way. No time for that sort of thing. Actually, I've got a few trips abroad in the next few weeks. You've got to make your sales pitch at the right time, you know. Got to be on the spot to snap up those jobs in Poland and Scandinavia. No, coaching's more in Jakki's line, I reckon.'

'Our boys won't go for a woman in that role, I'm sure of that,' Ricky retorted promptly. 'Different ball game that would be.'

'Yes, I expect you're right. Best of luck, anyway,' said Clark, thankful to escape back to his favourite TV programme.

That was just the stroke of luck he needed, Ricky rejoiced: the absence abroad of a man who might have been a problem at training sessions or when spectating from the sidelines. He had no doubt at all that the job would be his because he was surely the only qualified candidate. After all, he had been a player himself and had already done some coaching with the Kings.

His final phone call of the evening was to Josh's mother, Karen Rowley, someone he believed he would have no trouble in winning over to his point of view; but, as he'd proved many times in his own line of business, running a furniture factory, it was best to leave nothing to chance.

'Honestly, I really don't mind who's the coach just as long as Josh gets a fair deal, Ricky,' she told him. 'It's just so important to him to be in the team. You know, I think he gets more obsessed by the day, if that's possible. Just eats and drinks and dreams of football. Really, I don't think Sam has given him a fair hearing, a fair chance to show what he can do. Surely he deserves a regular place in the team. I mean, you'll want him in the team, won't you?'

'Karen, we need all the good players we've got,' was the diplomatic answer.

'Yes, but he will be *playing*, won't he? Not just a substitute? Sam had a dreadful habit of just keeping the subs on the bench. They didn't get to play at all in the match. That's sheer torture for a boy like Josh.'

'Er, well, he's in good form, I gather,' said Ricky, half-remembering a comment Alex had made the other day. 'He played a blinder in training, doing a tight marking job on the forwards. *Very* impressive, Alex said. So –'

'Oh yes, that's the time he got a nasty bang on the cheek. The bruise is only just fading. That's his trouble, you know: throws himself *headlong* into every situation. It's just his way. That's why he's convinced he'll score lots of goals if only he's given his chance. *You*'ll be able to do that for him, Ricky, won't you?'

'I'm sure he'll get his chance, Karen. I'll see to that. I mean, a team's got to be chosen on its merits, it's got to be well-balanced and, well, sometimes you've got to swap players around according to the opposition they're facing. So I'll just be doing my best for the Kings. That's what we've all got to do, isn't it?'

Karen wasn't entirely sure what he was getting at but, for Josh's sake, she had to seize every advantage she could. 'Listen, Ricky, if it'll help I'm perfectly willing to provide the team with new shirts and shorts. I mean, some of them are looking a bit worse for wear and, well, I'd like to do that. I'll even guarantee to wash them all after every match. That'll save other mums from having to do the chore. With two kids of my own the washing machine's always on the go so it'll be no extra effort, honestly. Will that help?'

'Wonderful offer, Karen, wonderful. Wish everyone thought as much about others as you do,' Ricky said. Now that he had escaped the trap of promising a place to a player he wasn't sure was good enough he could afford to sound enthusiastic. 'So, many thanks for your support. I'll be in touch again as soon as I take over as coach – always assuming that's what *does* happen.'

'Oh, I'm sure it will, Ricky. You've definitely got my vote,' she told him before he rang off.

Josh had been trying to listen to every word of the conversation but couldn't work out most of what Mr Todd was saying. '*Is* he going to take over the team, then? And did he say I'd definitely be playing?'

'He didn't make any promises, Josh. You can't expect him to at this stage. But he knows how I feel about things. And he did ring us, didn't he? He needn't have done. Oh, and even Alex has been praising you, apparently.'

'I expect he's just trying to make up for kicking me in the face,' Josh muttered. 'Alex doesn't care about anyone but himself. I expect his dad's the same. He'll probably make Alex the captain from now on.'

'Surely not! That's Joe's job, and Joe always seems to play well, doesn't he?'

'Joe's a defender. I'm a forward, a striker. Well, I would be if only Sam the Slam let me play. Ricky Todd's dead keen on attackers. That's where Alex plays. So he probably doesn't rate me at all because he hasn't seen me whacking the ball into the net.'

'In that case, you'll just have to make sure he *does* see you doing that,' his mum pointed out with her usual sense of logic. 'You'll have to do something special to impress him at training. Then you'll be in the team. I told him how important that is to both of us.'

Josh ran his fingers through his short, curly fair hair and then jumped to his feet. 'I will,' he said fiercely. 'I will. Even if I have to kick Alex to pieces to do it. I'm going to stop at nothing to get what I want.'

His mother smiled. 'Well, I'm sure you and Ricky Todd ought to get on very well together. You seem to me to be on exactly the same wavelength!'

3 Points of View

Even when he was on a bicycle, head down and pedalling hard, there was no mistaking the tall figure of Josh Rowley. Dominic Allenby, sauntering out of a side road into Rodale Kings' High Street, hailed his teammate and then watched in amusement as Josh, braking, skidded sideways and almost fell off. Josh glared at him as Dominic unhurriedly approached.

'You could have caused an accident, calling out like that,' Josh said accusingly. 'Never saw you.'

'Sorry,' Dominic said amiably. 'Can't do with any more injuries, can we? I mean, it's bad enough with the Boss being out of action and Danny's supposed to have damaged a finger playing volleyball. Risky game that, for a goalie, even if it does help your punching. Anyway, if you're heading for the match you're going to be a bit early, aren't you?'

'Maybe, but I don't want to miss anything, do I?' Josh replied, his cheeks a little pinker than usual. 'Want to make sure Ricky Todd puts me in the team from the start. Feel I'm going to get at least one goal today, probably two. Just a feeling, Dom, but it's *there*.' And he pressed a hand over where he believed his heart to be.

'Well, I hope you do, Josh. We've got to beat Stonecreek if we're going to win the League. Be funny playing under a new coach, though, won't it? He's going to have lots of different ideas from Sam, isn't he? He's bound to make changes all round, might drop *anybody* he thinks doesn't fit in with his "style". That seemed to be his favourite word when he talked to us on Tuesday night.'

'You don't have to worry about being dropped, though, do you? You're a certainty in defence. You won the man-of-the-season award and Sam said he'd never seen any player improve as fast as you did. So your place is guaranteed,' remarked Josh, trying to keep envy out of his voice.

'Josh, *nobody* can be sure of anything with

a new coach, not even Joe, and he's the captain. Maybe not even Danny even if he is the best goalie in the League, I reckon. Sam had to praise me because he'd converted me from an attacker to a defender and we all agreed it worked. And now I really *like* being in the back four alongside Joe and Kieren and whoever else gets picked. Like I say, things are going to be different under Ricky. Might even be new players coming in we've never heard of.'

Josh looked worried and when Dominic moved away to sit on the circular wooden seat that surrounded a chestnut tree he followed suit, propping his bike against a neighbouring lamp-post. 'I've done the opposite to you, moved from the back to being a striker. So I'm not, well, a regular yet, am I? If Mr Todd does bring in someone else I might have to fight for my place. But my mum's had a word with him and she says I should be all right.'

Dominic blinked. 'You mean you got your mum to ask him to pick you for the team? That's a bit sneaky, isn't it, Josh? I mean, we all want to play for the Kings but it's up to us to *prove* we're good enough.'

'No, no, it wasn't really like that,' Josh explained hastily. 'Mr Todd rang *her* first when he was trying to find out who would support him as the new coach. She said he was quite careful about it, didn't want people to think he was jumping in with both feet the moment he knew Sam was injured. Kieren says he rang them, too, and asked if Mr Kelly wanted the job. Kieren's dead pleased his dad said no! Oh yes, he also said if Mr Todd had asked his mum she might have said *yes*!'

Dominic had heard nothing of these manoeuvres and now he wondered whether Ricky Todd had been in touch with his parents. Although his father had little interest in the game his mum had taken to attending matches quite regularly. Because of her training as a nurse – she worked now as a midwife – she'd even been able to help out on the medical side when a player took a knock. Dominic wasn't at all sure that he cared for the presence of parents at a match but there was nothing he could do about it. Now it occurred to him that perhaps his mum, too, might have been willing to take over as coach.

She always claimed that one of her assets was that she was 'a quick learner', and so doubtless it wouldn't take her long to learn about coaching. However, Ricky Todd had the job so the matter was settled.

'Hey, just thought of something,' he announced to change the topic. 'What d'you think we should call him? Mr Todd, I mean. Wouldn't sound right to call him Boss because that's Sam's title. And "Mr Todd" sounds a bit feeble.'

'I wondered that but I don't know what's best. On Tuesday night I noticed nobody called him anything, except Alex and he just says Dad! Couldn't do anything else, could he?'

'Oh well, maybe we should ask him then and –'

'Hey, listen, Dom, it's time we were off. Told you, I want to be there early and –'

'Relax, Josh, relax. My mum's giving me a lift any minute now and she can take you and your bike as well. I only walked here because there's a camera in that shop over there that I really fancy for my birthday. Can't take my eyes off it! Mum said she'd pick me up in a couple of minutes and – here she is, right on cue!'

Jane Allenby's fire-engine red saloon emerged into the High Street and then slid to a halt beside the chestnut tree. She awarded Josh a cheerful greeting with a brilliant smile and then efficiently folded up his bike and stowed it in the boot. As they speeded up out of the village she glanced at Josh through her rear-view mirror and asked how he was feeling about the match.

'Oh great!' he enthused. 'Can't wait for it to start. I'm going to score today.'

'Not feeling nervous, then?' was the unexpected next question.

'No, told you, I'm OK,' he insisted.

'Good, good. It's just that I couldn't help noticing your eye movements. You seem to be looking everywhere at once. People who are really nervous do that sometimes. So –'

'It's my eye exercises; it's what I do to strengthen the eye muscles,' Josh explained eagerly. 'If I can make them stronger then I won't need glasses, you see.'

'You mean *you* see!' Dominic laughed.

'Should you be wearing your glasses now, then?'

'No, definitely not,' Josh snapped. He hadn't at all appreciated Dominic's little joke. 'But I don't want to miss anything.'

'Josh, don't worry about it,' Mrs Allenby said gently. 'You do what's best for yourself and the team. Now, who can tell me what the final score's going to be today?'

'Four-nil to the Kings!' the boys said simultaneously and then looked at each other with delight at having come up with an identical forecast. Nobody had suggested anything like that at Tuesday's training session so they felt the coincidence must be a good omen.

'I'm staying for the whole match so I'll give you a lift home afterwards, Josh, unless you prefer to ride your bike. Depends, I suppose, on how much energy you have left,' Mrs Allenby smiled as she parked the car close to the changing-rooms. 'Anyway, have a good game and don't take any risks.'

She always said that even though she knew they wouldn't remember a word of what she told them. Now she looked round the ground to see who she might chat to but so far hardly anyone else had turned up, apart from Ricky Todd, of course, and he was deep in conversation with a trio of people she assumed were the match officials, two men and a young woman. 'But I'll bet the girl isn't the referee,' Jane told herself, and she was right. But at least she was running a line.

'Good to see you! Hope we put on a stylish display to entertain you,' Ricky greeted her when he was free of official discussions. Although he now had the coaching job for the foreseeable future, he wasn't missing any chances of winning over personal supporters. He'd become aware that Jane Allenby was showing increasing interest in the Kings and so he wanted her on his side. Moreover, anyone with medical knowledge was always an asset to a junior team.

'Dominic believes you're going to win 4–0 today,' she told him to see how he'd react.

'Oh, I'll settle for that!' he responded cheerfully, although his eyebrows shot up. 'Stonecreek aren't a bad side, though. Don't think they'll roll over as easily as that. May be quite a tough game.'

'Typical coach! They all say every game'll be a tough one,' she murmured, although she added a smile to show she wasn't getting at him. Dominic would never forgive her if she antagonized the man who'd be picking the team from now on.

As she waited for the teams to come out on to the pitch and watched the arrival of more spectators she reflected on how football had helped to change her only child. Because both his parents had jobs that took them out at unsociable times, Dominic was used to being on his own and therefore fairly self-sufficient. But his success at soccer had definitely given him confidence; he was bolder and more positive in practically everything he did nowadays. And that self-assertiveness, she knew, was not down to his reddish hair! Ken, her husband, who also had a gingery tinge to his thinning hair, was as mild a man as one could find. His interest in sport was minimal, apart from his enjoyment of racing, so Dominic had to look elsewhere for support for his football fanaticism.

In the changing-room Ricky began his first official team-talk with the unexpected prediction, 'We're going to win 4–0 today. Or so the experts tell me!'

Dominic and Josh exchanged startled glances but didn't say a word. Was this sheer coincidence or had Dominic's mum been talking to the coach? Mr Todd didn't enlighten them or anyone else but instead went on that he didn't expect it to be as easy as that.

'But it's important we get off to a good start,' Ricky added. 'That'll give us all a boost, me included. Most of all, though, it'll be a tonic for Sam Saxton. He's sent you a good luck message and says he's sorry not to be joining us today. He still needs to rest his leg. So let's make sure we win this one for Sam. Go on, Kings, go and WIN!'

Ricky suspected that Sam wasn't being truthful about that; almost certainly he was being diplomatic in not turning up at his successor's first game in charge. He might also, Ricky suspected, be losing interest in the team for when Ricky had approached him about his taking over the responsibilities of coach, Sam had surrendered almost immediately. So the battle that Ricky had expected to fight for control hadn't taken place at all.

He'd got what he wanted in the easiest way possible.

'Dad, you have told Josh he's to keep pushing the ball through to me, haven't you?' Alex murmured as the two of them left the changing-room side by side. 'You know he hasn't got any pace, so he'd be useless tearing off towards goal on his own.'

His father frowned. 'Alex, I want you to help *him*. He'll be doing everything he can to get goals for us, you know that. But he's got to get into the role because he's mostly played at the back. He can jump and he can head the ball and he might turn out to be very good. So we've got to be patient.'

Alex had never been patient about anything in his life but he'd learned not to argue with his dad; he merely repeated his own point of view as often as possible. 'Well, if he isn't doing any good put Davey on. He's desperate to get back into the team. Sam never gave him much of a chance, you know.'

Ricky thought about that as the teams warmed up for a few moments before the ref summoned the skippers to the centre circle. If he hadn't given his word to Karen Rowley that Josh would play against the Pirates he'd probably have chosen Davey to play up front with Alex. On the other hand Davey, like Alex, wasn't the tallest of players and the Kings needed some height up front. Josh could certainly provide that. Still, it was always good to have a player on the subs' bench who believed that the moment he got on to the pitch he'd win the game for his side. Like Alex, Davey lacked nothing in confidence in his own abilities.

The new coach's other major change was to bring in Matthew Forrest as a back-four defender. That, he recognized, might be a gamble, for Matthew had little pace and not much more positional sense; his chief contribution, therefore, should be the strength and accuracy of his kicking. Perhaps, too, playing alongside Joe Parbold and Kieren Kelly would inspire him to develop his game. Anyway, a coach had to experiment and try out new ideas or what was the point of taking on the job in the first place?

Joe, the Kings' captain, won the toss and decided that they should kick-off, a move that surprised their opponents who really didn't care which way they played first and so settled for the half they were already occupying. In their navy-blue and yellow quartered shirts and blue shorts, Stonecreek Pirates looked as neat as their football in the opening minutes. Josh, over-eager to attack the moment he had possession, tried a mazy run and quickly lost the ball to an opponent who skilfully hit a long pass to his winger. And the winger swerved past Matthew Forrest with depressing ease before sending in a high cross that was cut out by the athletic Danny before any damage was done.

To his credit, Alex didn't say a word about the pass he felt he should have got and didn't and Josh simply vowed to make better use of the ball next time he got it. Foggy Thrale, playing just behind the strikers and ordered by his new coach to stay in the middle and not wander to the flanks, was keen to make an impression, too. He was another player convinced that Sam didn't recognize his talents. Under Mr Todd's direction, however, he expected to flourish if only he could get possession.

Stonecreek showed the greater composure

in the early stages. Their winger's successful foray past Matthew Forrest wasn't missed by their coach, who sent out signals to concentrate their attack down that flank. The team's playmaker, Reuben Jones, had a left foot that was the admiration of every coach in the Highlea Sunday League for he could pinpoint a pass practically on to a pound coin. And, after noting Matthew's ponderous movement off the ball, Reuben began to torment him with a stream of passes to his speedy winger.

'Stay with him, Tree, stay *with* him!' Ricky yelled to his defender: but Matthew hadn't a hope of that once his opponent accelerated.

Inevitably, the opening goal came via a pass from Reuben that, this time, the winger chipped into the middle with his first touch. The speed of the manoeuvre took even Joe by surprise and before he could head the ball clear, a Stonecreek striker hurtled in at breakneck pace to knock the ball down and then, left-footed, sweep it beyond Danny into the net.

'Oh no!' Ricky's hands went up to press against his temples. Within a quarter of an hour of the start of his first match as coach, his side was a goal down: and it wasn't the result of bad luck, simply bad defending. Now he had to decide what to do about it. His first instinct was to replace Tree Forrest but that might not be the answer. The sub who was there for defensive duties was in-experienced as a back-four player and Ricky had selected him as someone to swap for a midfielder later in the game if necessary. So a change of formation would be a better plan: Kieren, altogether more mobile, and Tree could change places.

'Come on, Kings, get cracking!' Ricky urged them as the minutes ticked by towards half-time with no improvement in the team's sluggishness. What on earth's wrong with them? he kept asking himself. But he couldn't see the answer. He tried not to wonder what Sam would do in this situation.

Alex was the first player to give the sup-porters some hope that things would improve after he picked up a lob from Foggy and tried a shot on the turn from just outside the box. It was highly speculative but the goalkeeper, taken by surprise, couldn't do better than palm the ball over the bar. Joe and Kieren came up for the corner but Josh was the one who got his head to the ball, sending it crashing against an upright from where it was scrambled to safety while Josh picked himself up from the floor.

Jane Allenby, watching intently, vigorously applauded the shot and loudly called, 'Well done, Josh! Keep going!' In physical terms he was a complete contrast to her stockily-built son. Josh, thin and angular, looked as if he'd already outgrown his white shorts and even his purple and white shirt looked too small for him. More than anything else she wished that he would score a goal but he didn't seem to have a lot of energy. Perhaps he was out-growing his strength as well as his football kit.

It was an isolated raid and, soon, the Pirates were attacking again, although this time the tricky winger was finding Kieren harder to outwit. Twice Kieren judged his tackle to perfection and came away with the ball, much to the disgust of one of the visiting fans, a florid-faced man in a yellow and blue anorak.

'Go on the outside, Liam. You're not thinking, son! Do it right,' he yelled, even stepping over the touchline so that he could get closer still to the boy. Then, barely a minute later, when Liam again failed to make progress and allowed Kieren to snatch the ball away from him the Pirates' supporter gave voice again, 'You're useless, Liam, useless! Use your brains – push the ball the other way – nutmeg him – do *something* right!'

Jane Allenby, standing close by, saw that the boy was actually flinching as the man berated him. His game had gone to pieces and that wasn't because of Kieren's tackling and marshalling skills. She began to dread what might happen next time when the ball came his way, and, sure enough, Liam made a complete hash of trying to control a pass and the ball went out of play for a Kings' throw-in.

'You're *worse* than useless, Liam: complete *rubbish,*' the anorak man stormed. 'If you can't trap a ball you might as well get off the pitch right now.'

Liam turned away, his face scarlet. Jane's sympathies were aroused and she couldn't remain silent.

'I thought the boys were here to *enjoy* their game,' she told the man. 'He can't be enjoying anything, the way you're going on at him.'

He barely deigned to look in her direction as he answered, 'No, they're not here for enjoyment. They're here to *win*.'

Jane was too surprised to respond to that immediately. She'd feared he would turn his abuse on her and she'd been prepared for that; a declaration that nothing mattered apart from success was harder to deal with but she was used to coping with people, usually patients, who weren't in control of their senses.

Before she could say anything, the man, after shooting a quick glance at her, added, 'I was unlucky at football but my lad's not going to be like that. He's got to learn how to overcome problems on the pitch the hard way. There is no other way.'

Then, as if he'd said all he was willing to say, he turned and walked several paces along the touchline. Jane, still surprised at learning that Liam was the man's son, could hardly follow him to continue the exchange. Clearly it was a matter that could only be sorted out within the family or with the help of the Pirates' coach, who, surely, knew what was going on.

With just seconds to go before half-time Stonecreek doubled their lead. Once again, Reuben Jones, the fair-haired midfielder, set the attack in motion with another pinpoint pass from a deep position. This time, though, he ignored Liam's presence and fed the striker, who neatly lobbed the ball over Joe's head as the Kings' skipper advanced to close him down. With startling acceleration the striker then raced unimpeded for several metres before unleashing a long-range shot. Danny, loitering at the edge of the box, saw too late what might happen. Even as he spun to try to cover his goal the light wind that was blowing across the pitch carried the ball just inside the far post and into the net.

The scorer, who hadn't really believed he'd got a chance of a goal, turned a double somer-sault to express his sheer delight. Reuben merely held both arms aloft like a boxer who's delivered a knock-out blow.

'I really can't believe what I'm seeing,' Ricky Todd told his silent players at half-time. 'We're just presenting the game to the opposition *on a plate*. Nobody, nobody at all, is doing anything to win it for us. You're not playing like Kings, you're playing like clowns. Idiots!'

He'd worked out that phrase earlier in the week but expected to use it only in a desperate situation with the aim of galvanizing the players; he was appalled he was using it already. He knew that Sam rarely tongue-lashed his players but Ricky believed there must be a time for it. Sarcasm sometimes succeeded in certain situations.

'Coach, I'm sorry about that floater I let in. Didn't think he'd try a shot from that distance,' Danny apologized. He'd decided that Mr Todd was the sort of man who'd like to be called Coach rather than Boss; and he was right. 'Won't happen again, honest.'

'Danny, it's not you I'm getting at,' was the smiling response. 'Just a freak, their second goal. No, it's the players in front of you who're letting us down. Who agrees with me? Who *knows* he's playing badly?'

Nobody said a word. Nobody felt he'd made a mistake as bad as Danny's. Nobody wanted to be regarded as a sycophant who would admit to anything simply to get on the right side of the coach. Everybody resented being described as an idiot.

Ricky sensed that his leadership was being tested. The silence slightly unnerved him because he'd expected to deal with someone's admission of guilt. In their family life Alex was inclined to argue with him about most things where they held differing views but it was clear none of the Kings felt able to express opinions at present. They were waiting for him to tell them what to do, and, he reasoned, they'd do it if it was within their powers.

'We're letting their creative midfielder, that fair-haired boy with the good left foot, dictate play,' he said carefully. 'So he's got to be marked out of the game and that'll give us a chance to open things up. Marc, I want you to stick to him like super glue. Close him down completely.'

'Me!' Foggy looked horrified. 'I'm an attacker, not a defender. I'm supposed to back up the strikers. I mean, I should be a striker myself and –'

'Marc, that's an order. I want you to do it for the team, understand?'

Foggy swallowed his objections. Coaches *never* seemed to know what he was good at and they wouldn't let him tell them. 'Er, right, Boss – Coach, I mean,' he muttered.

'Lloyd, I want you to be more mobile, get about and tackle like a – a tiger,' he told the midfielder, Foggy's usual partner. 'You've got pace, so use it for everything. Same goes for you, Josh. You're playing far too static a role, waiting for the ball to come to you. It won't. You've got to go for it, *die* for it, use it. OK?'

Josh, too, thought he was being picked on, revealed as one of the culprits responsible for the Kings' poor showing; and he also believed that wasn't fair. He wanted to ask why Alex wasn't being told the same thing. In Josh's eyes Alex had been no more successful than himself: worse, really, for at least Josh had hit the post and might easily have scored.

'Josh, you did really well, you were *so* unlucky not to get a goal!' a sympathetic voice interrupted his unhappy thoughts.

'Oh, er, thanks, Mrs Allenby. But I'm going to get one in the second half, *definitely*.'

Her smile hadn't faded. 'Good for you.'

Now that Mr Todd had moved away for a word with Joe and Kieren, Foggy sounded off. 'Why do all coaches think I'm a defender?' he asked anyone who'd listen.

'Because you're not a striker,' Alex told him bluntly.

'Oh yes I am! I can score fantastic goals if I get the chance. Your old man ought to know that. He's seen me do it plenty of times. But he only watches you, doesn't he, *daddy's* boy?'

'Hey, keep your voice down, Foggy, he's bound to hear you,' Dominic advised.

'Well, I don't care *who* scores for us just as long as we win this match,' Alex said quietly and one or two of his team-mates blinked in surprise that he seemed so much concerned with the team's rather than his own performance.

'That's because it won't look good for the new coach if he starts off with a defeat,' Foggy pointed out unarguably.

Several supporters were saying much the same thing and Jakki Kelly, who'd arrived late because a friend had delayed her on the telephone, was already preparing her report

61

for Sam Saxton. She still wished her husband, Clark, hadn't rejected the idea of taking over the coaching himself when Ricky rang. Ricky, she was convinced, wanted the role for his own glory and that wouldn't benefit the team. All the same, the last thing she wanted was defeat for the Kings. They all cherished the idea of adding the Championship trophy to the Knock-out Cup they'd collected the previous season.

By the time the second half began, the wind had strengthened and was blowing favourably for the Kings as Joe discovered when he cleared his area with a kick that sent the ball all the way to the centre circle – yet he'd actually been trying to find Marc on the left side of midfield. Lloyd, sensing a chance to show he'd absorbed the coach's instructions, ran and leapt for it, nudging an opponent out of the way as he gained possession. To his relief the ref didn't object to the contact and Lloyd swept into the opposition's half. His intention was to run as far as possible before parting with the ball and so he ignored Alex's screech for a pass. Josh, sensibly, was veering away on the right flank, pulling a marker with him. Still the Stonecreek defenders backed off, certain that the bushy-haired midfielder, who'd never ventured so far before, must pass at any moment. Lloyd slowed down, toying with the ball, switching it from foot to foot, apparently taunting the opposition to try and take it off him.

'Here, Lloyd, I'm here!' Alex, left arm high above his head, was calling, confident as always that he could inflict maximum damage in the goalmouth if only he had the ball. Another defender converged on Alex and, with splendid timing, Lloyd fired the ball towards Josh on the opposite wing. Anticipating just that move, Josh ran on to the high bouncing ball, pulled it down with his stronger right foot and made a direct run for goal. His nearest challenger had tried to intercept the pass, failed, stumbled and was in no position to catch the tall striker. Josh was aware enough of what lay ahead of him to decide that his best option was to feed Alex, now charging into the box diagonally from the left.

'Well done, well done!' Ricky yelled from the touchline, just inside the Stonecreek half.

He could see a certain goal coming up if only his boys kept their heads. Alex really could not have asked for a better delivery as the ball arrived invitingly ahead of him a metre inside the box with most defenders now out of position. Alex had the entire width of the goal to shoot at as the goalkeeper hesitated over whether to advance or stay on his line. That didn't matter in the end because Alex, leaning back fractionally as he struck the ball, saw his shot crash against the crossbar. As the goalie turned to see what was happening the ball rocketed back into play. And Josh, following up at speed, got his shin to it and bundled the ball over the line.

It wasn't the greatest goal the Kings had ever scored but Josh was ecstatic. Alex was almost as excited because he knew that it would never have been scored if he hadn't hit the bar with a rocket of a shot. So he could regard it as at least half his goal. They danced around in a celebratory embrace while several of their team-mates rushed across to join in. Jane Allenby was as delighted as anyone and called, 'Great goal, Josh! Well done.' But she doubted whether he heard her.

Some spectators started chanting 'Kings rule, Kings rule!' The slogan hadn't been in existence long and so, when nobody else took it up, it soon petered out. It caught Ricky's attention, though, and he liked it, liked it very much. So he made a mental note to encourage its use at significant times in matches and on other occasions.

For the coach, the goal came at the ideal time. What's more, it seemed to him that the boys had carried out his instructions to the letter. So his tactical ideas worked! Nothing pleased him more than Lloyd's contribution. He'd always believed that the big midfielder had lots of talent but it wasn't often expressed; perhaps it was simply that he lacked confidence or needed to be *told* what to do. He remembered that the boy's mum, Serena, a single parent, had complained to Sam that Lloyd wasn't being given enough opportunities to show what he could do (Sam, at that time, had dropped him from the team because of what he saw as Lloyd's loss of form). It hadn't occurred to either coach that Lloyd just might feel overshadowed by the ebullient Foggy Thrale, who usually tried to do the things that Lloyd had just proved he could do at least as well.

Ricky was genuinely pleased for Josh and wished only that Karen Rowley had been present to see the goal. Until that moment, however, Josh hadn't really done very much. But then, he hadn't been getting the ball.

'Come on, Kings, we're back in the game – let's have the second one,' the new coach yelled at the top of his voice, clapping his hands above his head. Sam's style during matches was to display little emotion and Ricky thought that was wrong. The team was bound to feel better if they could *hear* their coach's approval, when they could *see* at a glance how he felt.

The second goal wouldn't come, however, in spite of the renewed vigour with which the Kings were playing. Foggy was doing his best to obey orders and shadow Reuben Jones but the playmaker's skills on the ball, his twists and turns and spins, would have outwitted a better marker than Foggy. So the left-footed passes still launched Piratical raids down the inside-left and inside-right channels so that even Josh had to fall back on defence at times. Josh was determined to run his heart out so that the coach could see he was indispensable wherever he played in the team. It wasn't bad thinking, just so long as Josh was in the right position to create or seize a scoring chance when it came along.

'I'll get a goal for us, that's a certainty,' Davey Stroud announced when, impatient for action, he went to stand beside the coach. 'Just put me on, Boss.'

The last word was the wrong one to use to Ricky Todd, although Davey didn't know that. It had been in the coach's mind to make a switch but now he decided to delay it a little longer as the tide looked to be changing again with a positive forward run by Kieren Kelly.

'Keep going, Kieren, keep going!' Ricky yelled at him, and Kieren did so. He'd been on the point of slipping the ball sideways to Josh, who was pleading for it. Now he powered on until robbed by the inexhaustible Reuben. And Reuben, of course, found a team-mate with a precision pass – and the team-mate sped through the gap left by Kieren – and when he shot for goal only a breath-taking, full-length diving save by Danny prevented Stonecreek from adding to their lead. Ricky, clapping Danny's brilliance, sighed with relief. It had been a near thing and another goal now might have killed off the game for the Kings.

'Come on, Josh, let's have another goal,' Jane Allenby sang out, and Josh, delighted to hear such vocal support, responded immediately by challenging a Stonecreek midfielder for the ball and winning it. Inspired still by his earlier success he set off on a weaving run. Twice he fought his way out of clumsy tackles before answering Lloyd's call for the ball on the edge of the box. Very calmly Lloyd, pushing the ball one way and then turning back, waited for the right moment to cross to the far post. Not recognizing the danger soon enough, the Pirates' goalie only managed to get his fingertips to the ball and divert it away from the in-rushing Josh. He couldn't keep it away from Alex, who stooped to head it sideways. A confused defender tried to clear it, succeeded only in sending it spinning backwards towards the goal-line where Alex quick-thinkingly back-heeled it into the net for the equalizer.

'Wow!' exclaimed Ricky, relief battling with surprise in his voice. Alex, he knew, would claim the goal, and deserved it, but the coach didn't doubt there'd been a deflection that took the ball past the keeper. He looked at his watch: two minutes to go at most. Now it was up to the defence to hold out.

In truth, the Kings should have won the match with what proved to be the final kick, or, more accurately, non-kick, of the game. Lloyd, revelling in his new role, again sliced through the Pirates' unhinged defence, went wide, cut inside again and then squared the ball into the box for Josh. It was the perfect pass between defenders and Josh had a clear sight of goal from six metres out. He swung his right foot, missed the ball completely and fell on his backside. Defenders might have stopped to laugh but instead they scooped the ball out of the area just as the final whistle shrilled. Josh, mortified, was still on the floor, no one having offered him a hand up. Alex turned away in disgust, Lloyd merely looked sorrowful.

'Bad luck, Josh, can't be helped!' Jane called as he trudged from the pitch.

'No, it wasn't bad luck, I acted like an idiot,' the gangly striker replied inconsolably. 'I've let everybody down.'

Ricky didn't say that when the players gathered together in the changing-room; he didn't say half the things he wanted to because he sensed this wasn't the right time. But he had to send them away with something to think about before the next meeting. 'You were dreadful, collectively dreadful,' he told them as they collapsed on benches before starting to undress. 'So there won't be a man-of-the-match award because nobody deserves it. That shows exactly how I feel about the way you played. If we don't improve in the next match there'll be big changes, I can promise you. Between now and Tuesday night's training I want each of you to think very, very carefully about your own play today, what you didn't do. Think about what you've *got* to do so that the team, the Kings, improves.'

But in spite of all that thinking the team didn't improve in its next match, a scrappy

1–1 draw with Scarinish Town Boys. And the match after that was a defeat, a bad one, 1–3 to Bankhouse Invaders, a team they'd defeated 3–0 in the previous season's Cup semi-final.

In the eyes of many, the Kings were in crisis.

4 Driving to Success?

Marina Saxton sat in her conservatory and watched, fascinated, the changing expressions on her husband's face as he talked on the telephone. He was in the sitting-room so although she could see him through two sets of windows she could hear nothing of the conversation. So she'd have to be patient until he put the phone down.

'You're not going to believe this,' he began when at last he limped in and sat down in the cane chair opposite her.

'Try me,' she smiled, 'and I'll do my best to believe anything, however amazing.'

'Well, try this: Ricky Todd's gone and booked an open-top bus to parade the team round the village before the Cup-tie against Torridon. How about that?'

'What! But I thought the team was doing *badly*. They haven't won something I haven't heard about, have they?'

Sam shook his head, his eyes still registering disbelief at what Jakki Kelly had told him on the telephone. 'Seemingly Ricky thinks it'll boost the boys' morale. If they act like winners they'll feel like winners and *win*. I suppose you could call that positive thinking. Hard to fault the logic. But what if they lose? Going to look a bit of a fool, isn't he?'

His wife gave him a shrewd look. 'Puts you in a difficult spot, Sam dear. I *know* you can't bear the thought of your boys losing. But if they do Ricky'll have to pack it in, won't he? I mean, they haven't won a single game since he took charge, have they?'

'The tide'll turn, bound to,' Sam replied. 'There're a lot of good players in the squad. Just a question of getting the best out of them. Trouble is, Ricky will keep tinkering with the formation I established. Boys of their age like to be settled, not switching about all over the place. Damages their confidence, that does.'

'Would it be worth giving him a ring, exchanging a few ideas,' Mrs Saxton asked after a few moments' hesitation.

'No, no, I couldn't do that. Don't believe

in interfering,' was the instantaneous response. 'He wanted the job, was convinced he could do it, so he's got to get on with it. No, Rina, it's his funeral.'

'Sounds like a *celebration* to me,' she smiled. 'It might just work, you know. Then our ambitious Mr Todd would never surrender the team back to you. Think about that, Sam: what on earth would you do?'

'Start another team, provide 'em with some rivalry,' he said promptly.

Her eyebrows shot up. 'Well, *there*'s a thought . . .'

Karen Rowley stared hard at her son. 'I don't believe you,' she said flatly. 'I simply don't believe you.'

'Well, what's the point?' Josh said in his voice of defeat. 'I won't be playing, will I? I might get on the subs' bench but that's all. What's the point of being on top of a bus so that everybody can see you and think you're a hero when you're nothing of the sort. You're not even in the team. Waste of time.'

'Josh, you can't be sure of what's going to happen today and Mr Todd must want you there or he wouldn't have asked you,' Mrs Rowley said in a gentler tone. 'You've said yourself that football's unpredictable. Someone drops out and so you drop in. Could easily happen today.'

Josh stubbornly shook his head. 'Ricky Todd's gone off me completely, ever since I missed that last-minute goal against Stonecreek. Nobody lets me forget that. Ricky said *I* was to forget it but he didn't. Otherwise he wouldn't have stuck me at the back again, a *defender*. I'm not a defender. Then he dropped me altogether for the last match, didn't he? So now I'm nothing at all. Just a waste of time going on that stupid bus tour.'

His mother reached out and put her arms round him. 'Josh, my love, it's not like you to give up so easily. You're a fighter. Go out there and fight for your place. There's, well, nothing else bothering you, is there?' He shook his head but she wasn't certain he was telling the truth. So she went on, 'I was wondering, you see, if the fact that I'm washing the team's shirts is embarrassing you. Has anybody been, well, funny, about it?'

Again, he shook his head. 'Nobody's said

anything to me. Oh, except for Dominic. And he said his mum thought you were doing a wonderful job. Showed real team spirit, she said. Dominic's mum told him nobody ever saved her from a weekly chore like that.'

'Good! Well, if it helps the Kings' team spirit that can't be bad. The *team*'s the thing and you're part of the team. So don't let them down. Go on that bus and *vow* to win your place back.'

Alex's impatience was growing by the second. 'Dad! Dad, come on. Look, if you don't hurry we'll miss the bus. Great joke *that* would be!'

Ricky, pulling on his track-suit top, paused, biting his lip. 'You don't think this idea is a bit over the top, do you? Be honest now. The other boys tell you what they think, don't they? So don't hold out on me.'

Alex was astonished. He couldn't remember ever hearing his father express self-doubt before; and Alex was sure that's what it was. He himself was often accused of being over-confident but only he knew that sometimes that was the best way of concealing his worries.

'Dad, it's a great idea! All the other guys think so, too. It'll put us on a high – I mean, *really* high up on a top deck, looking down on everyone else. Most of us have never been on a bus with an *upstairs*, have we? So –'

'Right, it *is* a good idea then if everyone's looking forward to it,' Ricky declared, his enthusiasm renewed by Alex's support. 'I think it's also bound to give us an advantage over Torridon. They already know they're facing the Cup-holders. Now they'll see we have style and lots of support and we'll really look as if we're going places. Which we are! So they're bound to feel a bit second-rate. And that will work in our favour.'

'Just as long as we win, Dad,' Alex put in unwisely. 'We desperately need to get out of this bad run, don't we?'

'Well yes, of course,' Ricky agreed quietly. 'That's the most important thing. The *only* thing that matters, really.'

As gently but firmly as possible Dominic said, 'Mum, you don't have to go on the bus, you know. None of the other mothers are going to be there. Well, unless Mrs Todd turns up. But she hasn't been around much this season. Perhaps Mr Todd's banned her from getting involved with the team now he's in charge!'

'I get the impression you'd like to ban me,' Jane Allenby said, and she didn't smile as she said it. 'Look, Dominic, I'm entitled to be there. I am an official member of the squad now, you know.'

'You're the *physio*, Mum, that's all. In the top Leagues nobody ever hears anything about physios except when they run on to the pitch with pain-killers and sprays and ice-packs and that sort of stuff.'

'Maybe, maybe,' she responded, packing another handful of small packages into her medical bag. 'But I take my job seriously. That's what Ricky Todd expects. He wouldn't have appointed me otherwise. I'm his second-in-command, really. Which means you could even think of me as the Kings' deputy coach!'

'Oh, Mum, don't go on about it!' Dominic requested rather wanly. 'It's a bit embarrassing really. I mean, they all know you as my *mum*. So when –'

'Exactly! So they don't have to worry about having a stranger care for them if they're injured or taken ill. They know I *care* about the team, that I'll look after them as well as I hope I look after you. You've had no cause to complain that I've neglected your health, have you, Dom?'

'No, no, of course not. But, well, *they* might feel embarrassed about telling things about themselves because they'll probably work out that you'll then tell me. And maybe they wouldn't want –'

'Dominic, they're all boys of your age, they're all much the same in every way,' she cut in, smiling gently now. 'It's part of my job to see that there couldn't possibly be any embarrassment of any kind whatsoever. Nurses are just like doctors, you know: we make sure that what's private and confidential for a patient remains private and confidential. We share our knowledge of a patient with nobody, nobody at all. Is that understood?'

'I suppose so,' Dominic murmured reluctantly. He hadn't really expected to win this argument but he hoped he might persuade her to miss the bus trip so that he could enjoy it without fear of being told what to do or not to do. There were times when he felt she was over-protective towards him.

'Anyway, I'm looking forward to seeing things I've never seen before,' she resumed cheerfully. 'That's why I've been looking forward to the top deck. From that height we ought to be able to see just about everything in the village. Maybe at last I'll see what Annie Chanter is hiding in her back garden! She never lets a soul in there, I'm told, not even workmen doing jobs in the house for her. D'you know, Dom, I ought to take my binoculars with me. Then I won't miss a thing.'

'Mum! Please!' Dominic pleaded, horrified.

Two hours later Mrs Allenby had to concede that the bus ride wasn't anywhere near as revealing as she'd hoped it would be. True enough, the ancient blue and gold double-decker bus had trundled down Vicarage Lane and she'd been in a prime position to peer over the side as they passed along Miss Chanter's property. But the view was thoroughly disappointing. For the garden behind the mock-Tudor house owned and occupied by the former hospital almoner was bare of everything except a lot of unkempt grass and what looked like a dilapidated rabbit hutch. Could it be that Miss Chanter was just ashamed of its very ordinariness? Or did the hutch really contain some exotic pet that might take a nip out of a visitor's finger?

Jane buried her curiosity and began to share in the delight of the players as they pointed out various landmarks and responded to the surprised looks and hesitant waves of villagers and strangers. Plainly they were thrilled with the experience and the opportunity to show off the Highlea Knock-out Cup, just as if they were Arsenal or Liverpool or Newcastle making the most of their welcome from tens of thousands of fans during a tour of their home city after a victory at Wembley. Initially Joe Parbold had insisted that he should be one of the two players to hold it up all the time because he was the captain of the Kings. When, however, he discovered what a tiring business it was, he surrendered it to others.

'Look, that's my house, the one with the red door – and that's my room, the window with the football stickers all along the top of it,' yelled Marc Thrale. Because of its foghorn quality his voice could be heard far ahead of the route and so everyone turned round. 'Mum *promised* she'd give me a wave. So where is she? Mum, Mum, *Mum*!'

For once, though, the power of his voice didn't produce results and no one appeared at the windows or doors of the Thrale home. Disconsolately, Foggy stumped across the bus to study the landscape on that side. Soon his excitement rose again when he was the first to spot the massive oak tree that for more than a century had guarded the entrance to the grounds of the local school. But Foggy suffered another disappointment: no one else seemed the slightest bit interested. After all, it was Sunday and thus hardly a day to take an interest in the school.

As the bus slowly negotiated a tight turn out of Hollow Lane and then gathered speed again past the new leisure centre Danny Loxham, raising the Cup above his head for the benefit of spectators with cameras, launched into the new chant, 'Kings rule! Kings rule! Kings rule!'

'This idea of yours seems to be paying off, Ricky,' Jane observed. 'They're enjoying every minute of this. It's also attracting plenty of attention from the locals.'

'And further afield, I trust,' beamed the Kings' coach. 'One of the Press photographers assured me the pictures will get into the county papers and maybe the nationals as well. He said it'll definitely catch a lot of interest because it's *different*, a team on a triumphal tour *before* playing the match! Good publicity never does any harm, does it?'

Jane smiled wryly. 'I'm sure you're right, which no doubt is why your company's slogan is emblazoned along the sides of the bus. Must say, I've always thought it quite neat: "Are you sitting comfortably? I am. So visit Todd's Furniture Factory for the best seats in the house!" Easy to remember.'

'You don't think it sounds a bit smug? A customer said that once.'

'Well, perhaps a little smug,' Jane agreed. 'But who cares if the message gets across?'

'Exactly my sentiments!' he grinned. 'Tell me, what're your thoughts about today's game? Now you're assistant coach you've got to contribute some tactical advice, you know.'

'Oh.' Jane's eyebrows shot up. 'I thought that was your department. I wouldn't want to go against your ideas.'

'I'm sure you won't, Jane. But as you've become so keen on the Kings I'm sure you'll have noticed things that've escaped me. Coaches often stick rigidly to their preconceived plans for players. Maybe we aren't as flexible as we ought to be. Really, I'm just letting you know that I'm always open to new ideas. I'm willing to try anything that'll help the Kings win. Sam didn't encourage co-operation, not really. I'm different.'

'I'll remember that, Ricky. So thanks for the invitation. Just one tiny thing: poor Josh is looking miserable these days. I know he's not been playing well and I'm sure you're right to rest him for this match. Well, drop him to sub, anyway. Now might be the perfect time to say an encouraging word, cheer him up a bit by telling him he's still in with a chance of getting on the pitch today. *If that's true . . .'*

'Good thinking! I know how Alex used to feel when Sam kept him on the bench or when he was pulled off during a game. I've got a lot of time for Josh. Just a pity he's lost his form. Right, I'll do it this minute.'

Now the bus had reached the garden centre, The Roots of Rodale, which was adjacent to the football ground, and nearly every member of the squad had rushed to the front to see whether any spectators had turned up.

'Hey, look at all that lot!' Joe exclaimed. 'Must be hundreds, well, *one* hundred, anyway. Never had as many fans as this. And loads of 'em with cameras.'

'Yeah, but they aren't *all* our supporters,' Lloyd pointed out. 'That must be Torridon's minibus over there. Oh yes, and that's their team. I recognize William Horleigh. Used to be at my school. Plays as striker. Not bad, either.'

'Well, they look *awestruck* to me,' remarked Ricky Todd, who'd come to peer over their shoulders after his comforting words with Josh.

'Awestruck? What's that mean?' Foggy wanted to know.

'It means amazed and flabbergasted and, well, envious. Yes, can't believe how great the Kings look in their special bus,' Ricky answered. 'They're bound to feel second-rate after seeing us up here.'

'Yes!' Foggy boomed. 'Kings rule! Kings rule!'

His team-mates joined in until Ricky said it was time to get off the bus and get down to playing football. As they clattered down the staircase Josh missed his footing and would have fallen but for being grabbed by Foggy, just ahead of him.

'Hey, you can forget that idea, Josh – knocking me out to take my place!' he chortled. 'I'm going to get the winner for the Kings today.'

'No you're not, I'm the goal-scorer and I'm going for a hat-trick,' Alex claimed.

But the promises and the boasting had to be put aside for a few minutes because the entire team, along with Ricky Todd and Jane Allenby, were required to line up for pictures to be taken in front of the bus. Ricky, after making sure that his company's advertising slogan was going to be visible as well, told them all to smile.

'Look like winners,' he added. 'We've got the Cup and we're going to keep it!'

The Torridon players and their supporters were silent witnesses, resisting temptations they may have had to jeer at opponents plainly rejoicing in their possession of such silverware. Then, when the photography was all over and the Kings were free to go and get some ball-practice before the game began, Jakki Kelly stepped forward and asked them to wait for a moment.

'I have a message for you,' she announced. 'It's from Sam Saxton. He wants you to know that he's thinking of you and wishes you all the best for your defence of the Cup. He says he's sure you'll have a great game and he'll see you again soon.'

None of the players made any comment as they broke away and ran on to the pitch but Jane smiled and remarked to Ricky, 'That was nice of him, wasn't it?'

Ricky raised one eyebrow, one of his ways

of expressing disbelief. 'Bit devious, don't you think?'

'*Devious?*'

He nodded. 'I'm sure it's his way of reminding everyone that *he* won something and we haven't won a single game yet. He didn't send the message through me, did he? I haven't heard a word from him since I took over.'

'Oh, see what you mean. Well, this is the game to prove we *can* win, right?'

'Definitely, Jane. If the Kings lose today I suspect Sam will want to come back in charge, injury or no injury. I wouldn't like that and I don't think you would, either. I get the impression you enjoy having a definite role to play for the Kings. Right?'

'Absolutely!' She turned towards the pitch. 'Come on, Kings!' she called. 'Rule!'

5 Penalty!

From the kick-off the Kings did their best to obey their assistant coach's orders. Alex, picking up a neatly chipped pass from Foggy, swept out to the right, exchanging one-twos with Davey Stroud before hitting a long pass for Lloyd Colmer to run on to down the right flank. For his part Lloyd took on the full-back, turned him one way, then the other, and then cut inside, accelerating as he did so. Davey, cleverly dropping off his marker, called for the ball – and got it.

Davey was determined to show that he deserved his promotion as Alex's striking partner. He believed that if only he could score a couple of goals in a game then Ricky Todd would never leave him out again. Goalscorers, he'd heard often enough, had to be selfish at times to get what they wanted, so he was going to do things his own way. Now he ignored Alex's call for a pass and instead surged through the middle, riding a couple of half-hearted tackles. Only when he was just inside the box did he release the ball, slipping it to his right for Alex. Unfortunately Alex, who'd expected his partner to continue going it alone, was just too slow to make the most of it. When he tried a shot it was blocked but at least the ball went over the by-line for a corner.

'Good start, boys, good start! Well done, Davey!' Ricky yelled his encouragement.

Alex, who clearly heard every word, didn't think much of that praise. He was convinced he'd have scored easily if only Davey had released the ball sooner. He shouldn't get a pat on the back for that.

In spite of his lack of height, Davey, chunkily-built, had a real spring in his calf muscles and he rose higher than anyone to reach the ball from Matthew Forrest's corner kick. All that was wrong with his attempt on goal was his direction, for it was near enough to the keeper for the Torridon player to knock the ball up and catch it as it came down. Then, when Alex, in his frustration, charged the goalkeeper the ref awarded Torridon a free kick for the infringement.

'Bad luck, Davey, but you'll score next time,' Jane Allenby sang out. Davey beamed. He guessed that Mrs Allenby and Ricky Todd were becoming friends and so it was a good sign she was watching him closely. If Mr Todd missed anything perhaps she would point it out to him.

Dominic had never known his mother shout like that at a football match or, really, anywhere else. But it emphasized how keen she was becoming on the Kings and he wondered how it might affect him. Would any of his team-mates resent the fact that his mum was part of the management nowadays? After all, one or two were unhappy about making comments in front of Alex in case he passed them on to his dad; and his dad made use of that information. Dominic, who hadn't touched the ball once so far, sighed. Life with the Kings had been much simpler when Sam was in charge: no one in the squad was related to him. Dominic had made great progress since Sam converted him from striker to defender and it worried him that

Ricky might not view him so favourably. Of course, his mum might be influential in that respect but she also prided herself on her sense of fair play. So she might feel it would be wrong of her to intervene on her son's behalf.

So Dominic remained confused. But, when the ball reached him from a failed attempt by a Torridon attacker to control a pass, he dealt with it as efficiently as usual and sent Lloyd off on another of the winger's searching runs down the flank. With Kings' supporters beginning to roar him on, Lloyd suddenly cut inside, swerving cleverly between converging defenders and his pass for Alex to run on to was judged perfectly. Alex had every incentive to keep going forward as the defender ahead of him seemed to have only one thought in mind: to back-pedal. That suited the pacy, combative, dark-haired Kings' striker. With such freedom as this Alex was prepared to attack all day. He didn't need support. Davey, he could see, had begun a decoy run to the right-side of the box while Lloyd was chasing in behind him to pick up any back-heel, a manoeuvre that

Ricky had impressed on them ought to be tried more often.

Without warning Alex suddenly changed pace, flicking the ball to one side of the retreating defender and then zipping past him on the other side as the boy literally didn't know which way to turn. Now that he had clear sight of goal Alex didn't delay by so much as a split-second, unleashing a ferocious right-foot shot which flashed across the face of the goal. But instead of entering the net it struck the base of the upright and rebounded into play. Davey, with a poacher's sense of finding the right spot at the right time, had already changed direction again and so was there to slide the ball past the stranded keeper.

With a dervish-like leap and twirl he celebrated his first Cup goal so energetically that no team-mate was able to grab hold of him for a congratulatory hug. Alex didn't even try. He was furious that he couldn't claim the score for himself after hitting a shot like that. To add to his irritation, no one was acknowledging that he created the chance for Davey.

From a section of the Kings' supporters a

new chant arose, 'We're going to keep the Cup, we're going to keep the Cup. Oh yes we are, the Cup is ours!'

It sounded as if it'd been rehearsed but it hadn't. Jakki Kelly, who at one time was a lead singer with a rock group, had simply started it off and others around her joined in. Jakki was delighted: she wasn't going to be up-staged by Jane Allenby in her support for the Rodale Goal Kings.

The message wasn't missed by the players. Within a minute of kicking-off again, Torridon were two goals down. Once more, Alex was the provider and not the scorer. Once again, Davey put the ball in the net and could scarcely believe his luck in being in the right place at just the right time so soon.

The move started with a hopeful upfield punt by Joe and the ball was then missed by the Torridon defender who was still thinking about his failure to close Alex down. Lloyd, roving far and wide as he'd been told to, now turned up on the left and without any real objective in mind hooked the ball high into the middle of the penalty area. The high bounce took almost everyone by surprise including two defenders who failed to bring it under control. The exception was Alex. His sprint into the area got him to the ball as it came down again and with a sideways flick of his head he sent it on to Davey. With the keeper completely out of position all Davey had to do was nod the ball forward into the unguarded net.

'Can't credit that we've scored a goal as easily as that!' Ricky, wide-eyed, exclaimed.

'Exactly!' Jane agreed. 'But they all count. Isn't that what they say?'

Torridon, known like Wimbledon as The Dons to their supporters, looked shattered by the double strike. Even before their very young-looking coach began remonstrating with his central defenders, the players themselves were arguing about who was at fault. Plainly, no one individual wearing the white with scarlet sash shirt and scarlet shorts was willing to accept blame.

'Come on, boys, you've given 'em enough start now, so start *playing*,' one of their fans yelled to general amusement. No one in the Kings' camp knew whether it was intended to be a joke or not. So everyone assumed that the Dons *would* get better and therefore it would be harder to score in the remainder of the game.

'You're looking a bit glum, Josh. Are you all right? Not feeling sick or anything like that?' Jane suddenly enquired.

'Oh, er, no, I'm all right, really,' Josh replied. He couldn't admit that actually he did feel sick, but only in his heart. For it was plain to the sub that there was little hope now Davey would be replaced for any reason other than injury. Those two goals might have been the *easiest* anyone could have scored but they were bound to look good on Davey's record card. If he managed another then probably he'd be a permanent member of the attack for the rest of the season. So Josh felt he had every right to look glum. Perhaps his own season was over already. Naturally he wanted the Kings to do well but he also wanted success for himself.

Ricky, overhearing Jane's question, shot him a glance. 'Make sure you keep on your toes, Josh. You're not wearing much and you'll risk a chill if you just sit around. Better do some warm-up exercises in case I need you.'

'Right, Coach,' Josh said brightly, believing Ricky might call him on after all. So he started a series of sprints up and down the touchline. That alone made him feel better.

Their coach's reorganization of their defence had improved Torridon's performance for the marking was distinctly tighter. And rougher. Because he was now seen as the chief threat, Davey wasn't being given a millimetre to move in; and when he did receive the ball from a chip by Joe on the edge of the box he was scythed down immediately. He needed treatment from Jane's capacious medical bag and the offender got a yellow card.

'How does that feel now?' Jane wanted to know before helping him to his feet.

'I'll survive,' Davey muttered grittily.

'Well done,' she praised, running her hand across his cropped blond hair. 'But don't retaliate. That would just cancel out our advantage over them.'

Josh watched with reawakened interest as Davey hobbled back into the action. He just *had* to get a game to show Ricky that he would *always* score goals for the Kings. His eyesight problem, he was sure, was now a thing of the past; it had been solved. Even in the worst situation on the pitch it wouldn't recur. So now everything should depend on his football skills; and every day he worked on them, practising harder than he'd ever done. Surely he would get his due reward. Davey, everyone must see, was having trouble even in jogging; probably it would be impossible for him to *run*.

Alex, too, was feeling frustrated. Lloyd seemed intent on doing things entirely on his own and so the crosses weren't coming over; Foggy was obeying orders to patrol the midfield and not venture forward except when there was a clear-cut opening; and Davey was providing no support at all. Alex tried to catch his dad's eye but Mr Todd was more concerned about his defence as Torridon, beginning to find some form, pressed forward for the vital goals that would keep their Cup hopes alive.

At half-time the coach expressed his disappointment. 'You're relaxing because we're two goals up and that's no good. Two-nil is always a dangerous score. If the opposition gets a goal back the effect is two-fold: *you*

begin to w...
in the game and *they* know they're back
at you stronger...hance. So they come back
of ten get the equa...ever and five times out
changed to *panic*. A...because the worry has
...right?'

The boys didn't kn...
them to agree with him ...whether he wanted
anything. Alex hadn't bee...not so no one said
busy muttering to Davey, ...stening. He was
edly whether he was fit enoug...quiring point-
Davey wasn't pleased. ...to continue.

'I'm fine,' he insisted. 'The ankle's feeling
easier all the time.' It wasn't but he didn't
think Alex was entitled to know; any news
was sure to be conveyed to the coach.

'Alex, are you listening? This concerns you
as well,' his father said sharply.

'Yes. I've heard every word.' Alex brushed
his eyebrows so that he looked fierce.

Ricky doubted that but it didn't seem
worth pursuing in front of all the other boys
and with several parents within earshot. But
he made a mental note to speak to Alex again
when they were at home.

'OK, then, make sure you all keep working
hard,' he added to round off his pep talk. 'We

need at least one more g... ...nd we mustn't
concede *any*.'

That goal came wi... ...wo minutes of the
restart so that the s... ...d half began as the
first had done. Th... ...fference was that this
time it was scored... ...om the penalty spot. Joe
Parbold took Ri...'s words to heart and so
when the ball b...ke to him in Torridon's first
serious raid h... ran with it instead of simply
hoofing it upfield. Because he'd never
ventured over the half-way line before,
Torridon didn't see much danger in that: he
was bound to give it away or lose it. He
didn't. He kept going until he was well into
enemy territory and then very neatly laid it
off in a reverse pass to Foggy, who was eager
to join in the attack.

Davey's mobility had increased a little and
he was calling for the ball, but not as de-
mandingly as Alex. Foggy, thinking about
scoring himself, charged on into the box and,
after cleverly rounding a full-back, fired in a
rocket of a drive at goal. Unluckily for Foggy
the goalkeeper was in the way. But the shot
was too strong for him to do more than parry
it. Then, as the ball bounced towards Joe,

whose own forward run hadn't ended with his pass to Foggy, another defender desperately strove to clear the danger. His bad luck was that he swept Joe off his feet in the same instant that he reached the ball. The thump as Joe hit the ground could be heard for some distance.

Penalty!

6 Collision Course

Every Kings' player, and most of their fans, screamed for the penalty. They hardly needed to because the referee was already pointing to the spot. Alex had seized the ball before anyone else could and tucked it under his arm as he waited for Joe to be treated by Mrs Allenby. Joe was shaken and had grazed an elbow but there was nothing serious to worry about.

As he waited, Alex remembered the previous season's Cup Final when the Kings had won in a penalty shoot-out. He'd been one of the scorers on that occasion and he was positive he was going to put the ball in the net again. Davey hadn't been playing in that match and so wasn't an experienced penalty-taker. Even if he had been, Alex still wouldn't have relinquished the ball in spite of the fact that Davey was on a hat-trick.

Josh, too, was thinking about a previous penalty, the one he missed in an earlier shoot-out against Clocklane. In his eagerness to get on the score-sheet he'd grabbed the ball even though he wasn't on the list of players due to take the kicks. And he'd hit the upright instead of the net. Sam had been coach then and Josh believed that he'd never been forgiven for that failure. It had largely been responsible for the way both Sam and Ricky had treated him as a player by dropping him from the team just when he thought he'd established a rightful place. Now a tiny part of him hoped that Alex, too, would miss with his kick.

Of course, Alex Todd didn't miss. Confidence always high when it came to facing a goalie in a one-to-one situation, he took a long run at the ball and, right-footed, drove it high into the left-hand side of the net with the keeper a long way from getting even a finger to it. Alex wheeled away with customary exuberance and several of his team-mates went to share hugs of delight. Josh just grimaced but, for appearances' sake, shared in the applause.

It was from that point on that the rot began to set in for the Kings. There was no doubt that the third goal made them feel that the game was won, that they didn't have to exert themselves any more. Now Joe and Kieren Kelly began to roam further afield and marking opponents seemed to be of secondary interest to them. And, suddenly, Torridon struck back. Their fastest midfielder broke away from a mêlée in the centre circle and, like Joe at the beginning of the half, kept going. Now it was the Kings' defence back-pedalling, believing that real danger was non-existent. The lone raider, however, slowed down to await support and when that arrived all he did was exchange a couple of one-two's and then fire the ball past a surprised Danny Loxham. Danny had been unemployed so long that he'd practically forgotten that the opposition existed; or, rather, that was how he tried to explain away his inactivity to his complaining fellow-defenders.

Ricky was annoyed. 'I warned them, I *warned* them!' he told Jane, who nodded that she, too, was displeased with their lack of discipline.

Five minutes later Ricky was livid. For some moments he daren't allow himself to speak because of the language he might use. All the things he'd warned them about had obviously gone clean out of their heads. He couldn't believe his players could be so thoughtless.

Once again the trouble came through an isolated raid by the mercurial midfielder, who this time decided to go it alone after poor attempts at tackles by Tree Forrest and Joe Parbold. Then, when Kieren succeeded in wresting the ball away from his opponent, he attempted to pass it to Dominic: and carelessly didn't hit it hard enough. It was intercepted easily by a Torridon striker, who promptly transferred it back to the midfielder. He smartly lobbed it over Dominic's head for his team-mate to run on to and try a shot. At least, he *would* have lobbed him if Dominic, for some unaccountable reason, hadn't stretched up a hand and pushed the ball down.

Penalty!

'I can't believe what I've just done!' Dominic gasped to Joe. No one else could,

either. No referee, however, would be interested in an excuse about a unique brainstorm.

Torridon's skipper strode up, placed the
ball on the spot and shot it home off the inside
of the upright with nerveless power. Rodale
Goal Kings 3, Torridon 2. By now everyone
on the ground was checking how much of
the match remained. Answer: ten minutes.

Mr Todd turned to Josh Rowley. 'Get
warmed up, Josh, and do it fast,' he snapped.

'Yes, Coach!' Josh was thrilled. His hopes
had just about evaporated but now there was
a chance to do something brilliant, a chance
to stake an unchallengeable claim for a place
in the team *at the start* of the next match.

He shared a grin of sheer pleasure with
Jane Allenby and then, head down, hared
along the touchline, eager to show off his pace
and determination.

What Josh failed to see was that the
Torridon sub was doing exactly the same
thing. He, too, had been put on instant alert
for a possible last-minute inclusion in the
game. The boys, looking at the ground and
thinking only of glory, hurtled towards each
other on a collision course.

And they collided. The shock was greater than the injury to either but both fell, clutching their heads. Spectators who'd glimpsed what was happening laughed until they saw that neither boy was getting up immediately. Then came the rush to see what help was needed.

Jane, who'd been intent on the game, didn't at first realize what had occurred but the manner in which both boys were holding their heads was a story in itself. She knelt to examine Josh first, quietly asking about pain and dizziness and loss of vision. Her simple tests showed that concussion was unlikely; and the Torridon substitute appeared to have escaped that fate, too. His youthful coach was more amused than concerned and his interest in what was happening on the pitch never wavered. Moments later he sent on another sub and signalled to the boy in the collision to go and rest.

'Josh, are you sure you're all right?' asked Jane, worrying about a delayed reaction.

He nodded, and then wished he hadn't because of the pain that caused. 'It's nothing,' he insisted. 'Just a little bang on the head, that's all.'

Josh felt foolish. He couldn't imagine how he'd failed to see the other sub and he even wondered if the crash had been deliberate. But he knew that was a ridiculous idea. So perhaps his brain had been affected after all.

'Have you given up wearing glasses altogether?' Mrs Allenby was enquiring.

'Er, well, I don't need them any more, you see,' he said tentatively. He hoped she would not want to know more but she did. 'Well, it's a secret, really. I mean, I don't mind you knowing, or Mr Todd. But not Alex, not the rest of the team.'

'Josh, when you're a nurse you have to keep all manner of secrets,' Jane said quietly while giving him an encouraging smile. 'So anything you tell me will go to no one else.'

'Right, well, I'm wearing contact lenses,' he told her in no more than a whisper. 'They are good, really good. I can see perfectly. But I worry that they might drop out and then I'll be in trouble, won't I? I thought one might have come out when we banged into each other like that. But it didn't. D'you think that proves they're really good, Mrs Allenby?'

'I'm sure of it, Josh. I've several patients who wear them so you –'

But the excitement among spectators at what was happening on the pitch interrupted their conversation. Torridon were pressing desperately for the equalizer that would mean a shoot-out, extra time not being allowed. They had forced successive corners and, from the second one, Danny only just managed to scramble the ball round the post for yet another flag-kick. In the process, he'd been kicked on the arm and Jane was needed on the pitch to attend him.

'D'you want me to go on now, Boss?' Josh asked as Ricky Todd stared, frowning, at his captain and Tree, who appeared to be arguing furiously about something.

'No, no, son, I want you to stay where you are, get over that crack on the skull,' the coach replied almost absent-mindedly. 'I'm going to pull Kieren off and put Gareth in his place. Can't have Kieren wandering all over the place like he has been doing.'

Gareth Kingstree was the newest of the squad, a play-anywhere type whose family had moved from the south coast to a neighbouring village. Josh had never seen him as a threat to his own position because Gareth wasn't a specialist. But perhaps, Josh reflected bitterly, that was the wrong view; perhaps Gareth was exactly the kind of player Ricky favoured. No one had seen much of him so far and Danny had remarked that maybe he'd been accepted only because the word Kings was part of his name!

Now, as Jane returned after patching up Danny, the coach signalled that he wanted to replace Kieren with Gareth. Josh wasn't the only one feeling thoroughly let down. Kieren's face was a portrait of dejection while his mum, Jakki Kelly, took a mutinous step or two towards Ricky. She was convincing herself that he'd replaced Kieren only because she was known to be on Sam's side.

This time Tree managed to get to the ball before anyone else and his powerful header cleared the penalty area. Foggy, who'd obeyed orders to drop back and defend as if his life depended on it, took the ball under control and moved it towards the half-way line, making sure above all else that he didn't lose possession. To his delight he heard the ringing tones of Ricky Todd, 'Well done, Marc! Don't give it away, son.'

By now the Kings' fans were whistling frantically for the ref to blow his whistle for the end of the match; by their reckoning he'd already played at least three minutes of 'injury' time. In fact, the ref believed there was still another minute left and in that time it was the Kings who came closer to scoring. Foggy, inspired by praise, fed Lloyd with a glorious pass. Although by now almost exhausted by all the running he'd done throughout the game, Lloyd summoned up a last spurt of energy to race into the penalty area before squaring the ball to Alex; but Alex, who hadn't expected a pass, wasted the chance by shooting much too soon. The keeper collected it without difficulty and Alex stamped his heel into the ground with anger. He daren't risk a glance at his father.

Then, to the total relief of the Rodale contingent, the last shrill sounded. Several supporters ran on to the pitch to salute their heroes and celebrate a victory that might so easily have been snatched from their grasp.

The team, almost to a boy, looked dazed at first but then began to embrace one another and, hands high above their heads, applaud themselves.

'Just like the Cup Final last season. Thought we weren't going to get the right result!' Dominic gasped as he and Danny hugged. 'Hope it's not going to be like this in every round!'

'I don't care, just as long as we get *through* every round,' replied Danny. 'I really fancy the idea of building up a collection of medals. I mean, it doesn't look like we're going to get anything in the League, does it?'

On the touchline Jane Allenby picked up her medical bag and exclaimed to Josh, 'Wow! That was some match, wasn't it? Can hardly believe we hung on like that. Thought I was going to have a nervous breakdown! How're you feeling now, Josh?'

'Bit sick, actually.'

She looked alarmed. 'Really? Is it your head that's bothering you, or – or –'

But Josh was shaking his head to indicate that wasn't what he meant. 'Sick because I never got on to the pitch. I *really* wanted to play in this match. I'm worried that Mr Todd doesn't think I have a future with the Kings.'

'Oh, I'm sure that's not true, Josh,' she told him as gently as possible. 'He was going to send you on as a substitute, wasn't he, if you hadn't collided with the Torridon sub. So Mr Todd must have thought you were good enough then and that was only minutes ago!'

Josh nodded this time, and that didn't hurt either. Then, glancing across the pitch, he saw that the coach was shepherding his players towards the changing-room. 'I'd better go,' he said. 'The Boss is probably going to say something important.'

Ricky Todd began the moment he'd slammed the door shut behind him. 'Just what d'you think you were playing at? Not football, for sure. Were you trying to hand Torridon the game on a plate?'

Of course, no one said a word. Sam Saxton would have *told* them what they'd done wrong; he would explain where the faults lay and what needed to be done to correct them. Then he'd leave them to think about things before returning to the subject at the next training session. In his view, immediately after a game, when everyone was, or should be, exhausted by playing so hard, wasn't the time to analyse a game in detail. He didn't ask questions and expect instant answers. Ricky Todd did.

'So, where did you go wrong, Dominic?' he demanded.

'Er, well, I made a few mistakes, I suppose,' replied Dominic, surprised to be picked on so soon. It hadn't occurred to him that he'd had a poor game.

'You gave the ball away, that's what you did! And that's a cardinal sin. Giving the ball away means handing it to the opposition so they can *torment* us. Don't you all agree?'

He looked round the room, at the blank faces of the boys sitting slumped against the walls, not one of them looking at him. Even Alex was staring down at his boots as if he'd never seen them before. Ricky sensed that because they must all be drained he ought to delay the inquest. Trouble was, he didn't know how much time he'd got with them. He feared that Sam might return at any time and try to resume control of team matters.

'Joe, what were you up to out there? What

leadership did you display?' he enquired, switching the spotlight elsewhere.

Joe blinked and then rubbed a thumb over the nose that had been dented in his solitary game of rugby. Until this moment he'd supposed he'd had a fairly decent game; he'd even helped create one of the goals that won the match for the Kings.

'Er, I don't know what you mean,' he said quietly. His tone, too, suggested that he didn't understand why he was being singled out for criticism.

'I didn't hear your voice *once*,' the coach told him. 'The skipper is my representative on the pitch. I need a leader who not only leads by example but *encourages* and *directs* his team-mates when things go haywire. And they certainly went haywire in the last stage of the game, didn't they?'

This time nobody really imagined he expected a reply. By now they were getting used to his style. What they hadn't expected was his attack on Joe's captaincy. Dominic had never told anyone that he liked the idea of becoming skipper one day. The fact that his mum had become friendly with Ricky

Todd, and was also officially the team's physio and assistant coach, might just help his cause. On the other hand, it might make things more difficult because Ricky Todd wouldn't want to show what looked like favouritism to Jane Allenby's son. Then again, Ricky hadn't pulled any punches in finding fault with him in this match just because he'd lost possession. In Sam Saxton's reign Dominic had received the most improved player of the season award and he was sure Sam wouldn't have criticized him so openly for just one lapse.

Alex, too, had his interest sharpened by his dad's comments on Joe's play. For Alex still nurtured hopes of being appointed captain of the Kings one day. It was a subject he'd raised with his dad and, predictably, Ricky had pointed out that this wasn't the time to promote his son to that role; Ricky had already had enough people ranged against him simply because they didn't approve of his taking over from Sam. If he displayed such blatant favouritism they'd probably call a supporters' meeting to have him removed and Sam reinstated. So he'd warned Alex to forget about that ambition for the time being. But maybe, Alex speculated, his dad's attitude was changing.

'You know where you all went wrong, don't you? You gave up too soon, you thought it was all over, that you'd already got it won,' Ricky went on, replying to his own question this time. 'You gave up going for the fifty-fifty balls, you gave up *fighting* for anything. And that's why Torridon got back into the game. They almost won it.'

He paused significantly and then concluded, 'You've got to get rid of that attitude once and for all. You've got to keep battling for everything until the final whistle. If you don't we'll win nothing. Your season will be in ruins. And we're not having that. So, if you won't or can't do as you're told there'll have to be changes. Big changes. All right?'

Still no one said anything but one or two nodded and Joe, worried about the captaincy, managed a hint of a smile to show he'd been listening. He expected that the coach would want a word with him in private after they were all changed; but by then Ricky Todd had other matters to attend to and talk over with

117

his new assistant, Jane Allenby.

The players, shocked by their coach's outburst after they'd *won* their match, sat on for some moments, thinking about what they'd been told and wondering what changes he might make and who would suffer the most.

7 *Alternative Games*

Lloyd swooped past the hesitant Davey, reached the puck with the very tip of his stick, swerved left and then right and finally whacked the rubber disc with much of the power he possessed. It thwacked satisfyingly against the chalked line on the glazed brick wall before Alex could even begin to raise his stick to defend his goal.

'YES!' Lloyd roared, spinning through almost 360 degrees on his rollers.

'NO!' chorused Alex and Dominic.

'Of course it was a goal!' Lloyd insisted, rolling up to point to the tell-tale mark on the wall. 'Look, you can see where it hit. That's my –'

'No, it's not. That's where I had a near miss when *I* was shooting into this goal last week,' Alex retaliated. 'I should know, you all claimed it wasn't a goal then. So it can't be one now!'

Lloyd, leaning forward on his stick, looked round for someone who might support his word. His gaze fell on Josh who'd just arrived and was strapping on knee-pads and the crash helmet all the street hockey players had agreed they'd wear if only to help identify who was playing on which side.

'You saw that, didn't you, Josh? You saw exactly where it hit. These peabrains couldn't spot an elephant on an anthill!'

'You mean, *you* couldn't see an anthill under an elephant,' Alex guffawed. But Lloyd wasn't listening. He was waiting for Josh's verdict.

Josh really didn't want to get involved in an argument about whether a goal had been scored because whatever he said would disappoint somebody; and he was anxious to remain on the best of terms with everybody. The street hockey games had only just started at Kingfishers, a new, exclusive development of houses just outside rapidly expanding Rodale Kings. So far only a couple of houses were occupied and the rest were in various stages of construction, as were some of the roads and perimeter walls. Because there was hardly anyone about at night Kingfishers was an ideal place for their games: no traffic on the uncompleted roads and no householders to complain about the noise they were making or the risks they imagined from being struck by the puck, which had been cut out of an abandoned tractor tyre.

'Come on, Josh, I want to know what you saw!' Lloyd called impatiently.

'Look, I saw nothing, honestly. Wasn't even looking,' was Josh's way out of the situation.

'You're just chickening out of it!' Lloyd snapped. 'Just like you chickened out of climbing that rope in Kingswood last Saturday. You're scared of committing yourself, Joshy. So –'

'No I'm not! I'd cut my hand on the carving knife at home, remember. That's why it was bandaged. I'll *always* have a go at things. I'm just as brave as you, Lloyd.'

'Yeah, he is,' declared Danny Loxham, coming up with unexpected support. 'Josh'll dive in for the ball if he thinks he can get it however many guys are kicking out like mad. Just like you did on Tuesday night, Josh, when Tree jumped in and almost broke your leg. I noticed you weren't around to help out, Lloyd.'

'I'm a forward, remember,' Lloyd replied loftily. 'So I shouldn't be hanging about at the back like you guys. Your job's to get the ball upfield to me.'

'Wish I had a definite position – you know, a regular place in the team,' Josh said because that thought was always in his mind. 'The coach won't listen when I tell him.'

When Alex was present the players had all taken to referring to his dad simply as the coach so that any adverse comments weren't regarded as a personal attack on Alex himself; even Alex sometimes spoke of his dad in the same way nowadays when things were still going poorly for the team. Although he couldn't possibly admit it, he occasionally wondered whether it was the best thing for the Kings to have Ricky as their coach.

'Listen, you're *good* in defence, Josh. You're a natural at getting in there and clearing up,' Danny said.

'Wish you'd tell the coach that, Dan. Honestly, I do. I mean, I think I'm better as a striker but I don't care where I play as long as I'm in the team. It's crazy, really, but you know I only played in defence on Tuesday because Tree and Kieren are off with chicken-pox. Just hope they don't come back too soon!'

'Listen, it's time we got back to our hockey,' Lloyd pointed out. 'You guys are just wasting good hockey time. Football's for Tuesdays and Sundays, not now.'

'It's Saturday for me as well now I'm play-ing for the school team because at last they've spotted my obvious talent!' said Danny. 'Oh yeah, knew I meant to tell you this and plain forgot. Scott Leven, a class-mate of mine – plays for Scorton Aces – well, he got a phone call the other day from Sam, our Sam, Sam Saxton. He asked if Scott was interested in playing for another team.'

'What!' several of the hockey players cried in unison.

Danny nodded. 'I'm not kidding. Scott says Sam was a bit mysterious, wouldn't say exactly what he had in mind or anything like that. Just wanted to know how he felt about another team.'

There was silence as they all assessed the

news: if it was true, how did it affect them individually and would it make any difference to the Kings?

'You haven't heard anything, then, Alex? You know, from your dad?' Josh enquired.

'Definitely not. I'm not sure he'd've mentioned it if he knew that Sam was, well, trying to build a new team.'

Josh felt his spirits rising. 'Hey, d'you think Sam is really going to start a new team? You know, one to challenge the Kings. Hey, that'd –'

'He couldn't!' Alex declared flatly. 'No chance. You can't start up a new team in the middle of the season and expect to join the League. That'd be a crazy thing.'

'Yes, but listen, he could be taking over another team in the Highlea Sunday League, one that's lost its coach, maybe. Or, well, Sam could be looking for extra players to sign up for next season. I mean, we know you can't have a transfer to another team in the same League in the middle of the season. Once you're registered you've got to stick with your team.'

'Yeah, we do all know that, Dom,' Alex

said, irritated. 'I'm sure Dad would've said if any of the other coaches were pulling out. He hears stuff like that from his contacts, you know. Your mate must've got it wrong, Danny. Probably it wasn't Sam. It –'

'No way, Scott's smart and he doesn't get things like that wrong. He just didn't have the chance to find out which team Sam Saxton was talking about. As I said, Sam was playing it cool. But something's going on, that's for sure.'

'Look, I think we should have a break, have our chocolate now instead of later,' said Dominic. 'I didn't get any tea. Dad wasn't back from his van round and mum's on a special hospital course. So I'm starving. Come on, let's get into the conservatory.'

'But – but – we haven't sorted out my goal yet!' Lloyd protested.

No one was interested in that at the moment. Instead, they followed Danny into the unsecured and unfinished conservatory at the back of one of the bigger houses. It had become their own place and because the windows permitted them to see in most directions they felt safe there; it was where they had what they regarded as their half-time break and it had become a habit to eat bars of chocolate. Although every member of the Kings' squad was welcome to join them, whether they wanted to play street hockey or not, only a few turned up regularly.

'Hey, I needed that, feel heaps better!' Dominic exclaimed as he pocketed the wrapping paper after swallowing the last fragment of an energy bar.

Josh, sitting beside him on the crescent of low-level lockers that would eventually become a cushioned window seat, offered Dominic his own remaining segment of chocolate. 'My mum made a terrific tea so I'm not all that hungry,' he added. 'Honest, I couldn't eat another crumb.'

'Josh, you've got to keep your strength up. If you get any thinner you'll disappear altogether,' Danny remarked, sounding genuinely worried. 'I tell you, my mum worries about you. She said so last week.'

'Mine, too,' admitted Dominic. 'I'd forgotten that. But now I feel guilty for scoffing your chocolate.'

Josh wasn't embarrassed by such concern

because he had his own worries about his weight; he feared that any hint of excess weight on his frame might cause his coach to drop him from the squad altogether. Now, though, he felt heartened by Danny's support.

'Look, the only thing wrong with me is that I can't seem to convince Ric – the coach that I ought to be in the team. So, listen, if Sam *is* picking a new team d'you think I ought to let him know I'm, well, available? Or should I stick with the Kings?'

'What're you talking about?' Alex said forcefully. 'How can you think of leaving the Kings, Josh? We're going to win everything in sight soon. You know Dad's getting everything organized now and we'll be unbeatable.'

For some moments no one responded at all: it was a view not many people shared. Most of the team were aware that spectators at home matches were increasingly critical of the team. Ricky Todd had made a number of changes and now only a few of the players were confident they'd be in the team for the next match. Of course, the squad wasn't big enough to allow the coach much freedom of choice and the current chickenpox outbreak made things still harder for him.

'Just suppose, Alex, that Sam came back, took over from your dad, right? What would your dad do then – leave? And would you leave with him?'

That volley of questions from Davey Stroud was a surprise. Normally, he said nothing at all, he was the quietest boy any of them had met. So when he did speak everyone tended to listen. This time his words amazed them.

'Don't be stupid, that's never going to happen,' Alex retorted. 'My dad is giving everything to the Kings. He's even the team sponsor now, in case you'd forgotten. So he isn't going to let Sam Saxton take over again. Even if Sam wanted it. Anyway, Danny's story is that Sam is trying to start a *different* team. That's because he knows Dad's in *total* control of the Kings. There's no way back for Sam.'

Davey shrugged and nibbled at his chocolate, clearly not inclined to follow up that enquiry with another question. Danny, though, wanted to know more.

'You've heard something, too, haven't you, Davey?' he said. 'So, go on, tell us what you know.'

Another shrug and then, 'I was with Kieren on Monday night, before he knew for certain he had chickenpox. While I was there Mrs Kelly got a phone call from Sam, asking about Kieren. Said he wanted to see him playing again. Said he missed the Kings a lot. That's all, really.'

To most of them that item of news was confirmation that Sam Saxton was definitely up to something; and that something could just as easily be his return to the Kings as an attempt to start up a new team. Alex frowned but said nothing. But now he was wondering whether his father told him everything after all.

'Look, we've talked *enough*,' Lloyd said loudly, shattering the silence. 'Let's get back to the hockey. Let's enjoy ourselves. All this talk about Sam is just boring.'

Then Foggy arrived, his eyes alight with the pleasure of being able to give them a piece of news he was certain no one else had heard. 'Hey, heard the latest, you guys? Joe's got chickenpox now so he's out of the Denholm game for certain. This is becoming an *epidemic*, never know who's going to go down with it next. 'Cept me, of course! I had it years ago.'

His listeners looked at one another, a wide range of emotions reflected on their faces. Alex looked almost cheerful while Josh was trying not to display elation. With 'The Rock', as Joe was popularly known, removed from the heart of the Kings' defence there was surely no doubt now that Josh would get a place in the team. Even if he were wanted at full-back he wouldn't really mind. After all, he'd probably get the chance of going forward for free kicks and other set pieces and so have an opportunity to score a goal.

'Tell you something else,' Foggy went on after a gratifyingly long pause to watch the effect of his announcement. 'The Kings will need a new captain and I'm the obvious one. So you can all start practising calling me skipper!'

'Rubbish!' Alex exploded. 'I've got the best qualifications of anyone. I'm top goal-scorer and my da – the coach says I'm a natural, completely natural, leader. So –'

'Well, he would say that, wouldn't he?' Dominic observed, flicking back his mane of reddish hair, a gesture that often signalled his willingness to argue his case. 'He's your dad. But he's always saying he doesn't go in for favouritism and so nobody's place in the team is guaranteed, not even yours, Alex. The same thing applies to the job of captain. He wouldn't want to show favouritism. So you're out, mate! The defender's in the best position to be captain, like Joe. Forwards don't see half of what's going on in a game. A skipper's got to be aware of *everything*.'

Most of the other players, with the predictable exceptions of Alex and Foggy, thought Dominic was talking sense and if a vote had been taken immediately among them then Dominic would have become captain. Foggy, though, was concerned only with his own ambition.

'It's got to be me, that's totally obvious,' he insisted. 'I'm in midfield now, so I see *everything* and I get *involved* in everything. That's what a captain's got to do. Oh yeah, and I know how to *lead* a team. On my own, that is. I don't need my mum standing on the touchline to tell me what to do.'

'Foggy, you've got a loud voice and that's about all,' remarked Danny before Dominic had decided how to retaliate. 'But you use it just to call for the ball for yourself. You don't actually go round *encouraging* your teammates, getting them to try a bit harder or just saying something like "well done, Danny!" I'd appreciate that!'

Danny laughed as he spoke and one or two of the others smiled but Foggy, of course, wasn't in the mood for humour, suddenly the matter of the captaincy of the Kings was a deadly serious business as far as he was concerned. He turned to Josh. 'Look, Josh,' he began earnestly, 'if it comes down to a vote you'll support me, won't you? I mean, *you* don't want to be captain, do you, so you'll give your vote to the best candidate. Right?'

Josh blinked with the surprise of being consulted in this way. To him, it really didn't matter a jot who led the team just so long as he himself was one of the players. He couldn't see any advantage to himself whoever was chosen as skipper. So he just shrugged to show his indifference. 'I just want to make sure I'm in the team,' he admitted. 'I just want us to win things and I want to be part of it. I honestly don't care who's in charge.'

'Dead right there, Josh,' enthused Danny, who'd suddenly realized that he, too, had claims on that leadership. After all, his position as goalkeeper was unchallenged and his skills were praised every week. Goal-keepers weren't usually chosen as captain but then Danny didn't consider himself as just an ordinary keeper: he believed he was ex-ceptional at his job. Moreover, he was in a better position than most to see all that went on in a match. 'All that matters is how the *team* performs. So if I had the job of captain I'd make sure we all worked together for the good of the Kings.'

'Look, I'm bored with all this chat about stuff that's not important, not at this minute, anyway,' Lloyd announced, getting to his feet and swinging his hockey stick like a cricketer wielding his bat on the way to the crease. 'Let's get on with *this* game. Bet I score the first time I get sight of goal. Anybody want to take me on?'

'Hey, hang on, hang on!' Dominic said firmly and everyone, including Lloyd, paused to listen. 'This is just to answer what Foggy said about my mum because it was a load of complete rubbish. My mum comes to our matches to support all of us, to support the Kings. She's not there on the touchline to give advice just to me. Fact is, she *never* tells me how to play. She's learned loads of stuff about football this season but she doesn't go around showing off. She's there if we need her because she's a trained nurse and knows all about how to treat knocks and sprains and worse. So don't go knocking her, Foggy. One day she might save your life!'

'Waste of time that'd be!' Lloyd joked and this time they all laughed, apart from Foggy himself, of course. But even he managed a half-grin and a mouthed apology to Dominic.

So they trooped out of the conservatory and within moments Lloyd was trying to make good his boast to score for his side. He'd probably have succeeded but for a courageous intervention from Josh, who dashed across to tackle, his stick thrust out like a sword. The collision between them was fierce enough for Danny to wince as he heard the impact. Josh rolled over and over on the hard surface but, miraculously, got to his feet without a scratch.

'Hey, you should play like that in front of me on the soccer pitch,' remarked the Kings' keeper. 'You'd make my job a lot easier. Might not to have to touch the ball all through the game!'

Lloyd wasn't so lucky. When he got to his feet he found he daren't put his weight on his left foot. So he sat down again, peeling off his sock after removing his wheels. The side of the foot beside the arch was extremely tender but there was no obvious sign of damage.

'Can't be anything broken, the bone'd be sticking out if there was,' Davey said unexpectedly. 'Saw that happen to a guy at our school. His face was whiter than that stuff they plaster on broken legs.'

'Just have a rest, Lloyd. Sit the rest of the game out,' advised Danny. 'I'll give you a lift home on my bike if it's no better. OK?'

Lloyd nodded wanly, not trusting himself to speak. His greatest fear was that he'd be unavailable for a Kings' game and his place would go to someone else who'd play so brilliantly Lloyd wouldn't get back into the team. If the coach knew he'd been injured playing some other sport he might be black-listed for ever.

'Alex,' he called softly when there was a break of play. Alex, surprised, glided across to him. 'Listen, don't tell your dad what happened to me if I can't play against Denholm. OK?'

Alex, however, just frowned. 'Course I won't. Got a lot more important things to think about than your sore foot.'

'I'd've scored that goal if only Josh hadn't got in the way,' Lloyd muttered. But nobody was listening to him.

'Dad, what's going on?' Alex urgently wanted to know. 'Is Sam going to take over again? Are you packing up? And who's going to be captain if Joe is missing with chicken-pox?'

'Hey, slow down, Alex, slow down! That's

a lot of questions and I haven't got a clue about most of the answers – *yet*. Until you told me what you'd heard I knew nothing about any of this. Except, of course, that *I'm* not packing up. No way. I know the team haven't been terrific yet but things are improving steadily. Everyone agrees on that. Well, that's what they've told me.'

Ricky Todd paused to sip his coffee and spread marmalade on a slice of brown toast. He didn't much care to deal with personal matters at breakfast because that was when mentally he ran through the business of the day that lay ahead of him. But Alex's anxiety about the future of the Kings naturally had priority this morning. After all, Ricky's own position as coach appeared to be under threat.

'But what about Sam?' Alex persisted in a quieter tone. 'I mean, he's over his injury now – must be – so it all fits if he wants to be coach again, doesn't it? Honestly, I can't live with that, Dad! He'll chuck me out again just because I "sulk" over something. That's rubbish. I just don't hide my feelings, that's all. And –'

'Alex, hang on! Let's not get into that scene

again. Even if Sam did make a comeback I'm sure he'd see that you're really focused these days, that you're a thoroughly responsible player. So he'll have no complaints of that sort. But, frankly, I don't think that's his intention at all – to resume as coach, I mean. I'm sure he'd've had the decency to let me know first if that's what he wanted. I expect he's quite enjoying his break – having a lie-in on Sunday mornings, that sort of thing. He's been a coach for one team or another for a long time and probably he's glad to have the chance to recharge his batteries. Oh, and it could be that his injury took more out of him than he thought it would. He's not a young man. Must be ten years older than me at least.'

'OK, but we need to know for sure, Dad, don't we? So, well, are you going to ring and ask him or what?'

'That would be rather tricky. I don't want to put ideas into Sam's head if they aren't there already. Another thing: he might even jump to the conclusion that I'm *wanting* to give up as coach but not quite willing to admit it. See what I'm getting at?'

'Er, yeah, I suppose so,' Alex conceded while sounding distinctly doubtful.

'So I think I'd better try a different approach, perhaps sound out one or two other people to see if they know anything about Sam's intentions. I can always chase things up this evening.' He finished his slice of toast, swallowed the rest of the coffee and stood up. 'Must get going, lot of work to be done at the factory today. So –'

'Dad, just a sec!' Alex pleaded. 'There's the captain's job to sort out, too. Last night Dominic and Danny and Josh seemed to be ganging up together and I think they're going to ask you to make one of them skipper if Joe's missing against Denholm. But the job should be *mine*. I'm the best goal-scorer, I'd *die* for the Kings. *You* know that.'

His father nodded. 'I agree with all that but I can't choose you, Alex. It would be the most blatant example of favouritism you could find. They'd all think that.'

'But that's not fair on me!' his son protested. 'Why should I be the loser just because you're the coach? If I'm the best leader, I should have the job.'

Mr Todd gave him a wry look and a sympathetic smile. 'That's hard to dispute, Alex, I agree. So I'll think about that, too. I promise you this: whatever I do it'll be for the good of the Kings. That's the way we've *all* got to think.'

When Ricky was at last free to make further enquiries about Sam and his plans, he didn't have any doubts about who to ring first: Jakki Kelly. The previous season, when the Kings had problems in scoring goals, Jakki had played an important role in finding a new player for the team, a German boy who actually lived in France. Karl-Heinz was the son of an old friend of hers and when he stayed with the Kelly family he proved to be an outstanding striker, one who also struck up a good partnership with Alex. At that time Ricky believed he had struck up a good relationship with Jakki because they both believed in the value of attacking football; but then, for some reason Ricky didn't understand, Kieren's mum had switched her support to Sam, perhaps because Sam believed in putting the defence first and Kieren had become a very capable defender. If anyone knew what Sam was up to at present it ought to be Jakki Kelly.

First he asked about Kieren.

'Oh, feeling very sorry for himself, of course,' was Jakki's reply. 'No chance of playing on Sunday, I can tell you that. It's what you were ringing about, I suppose?'

'Well no, not quite that, Jakki,' Ricky told her while feeling as if he'd been caught out in some underhand trick. 'I mean, I always want to know how my players are if they're poorly or have been injured in a game. Listen, please give Kieren our best wishes and tell him his place in the team is safe. Expect that'll help his recovery no end!'

'If only . . .' Jakki murmured, making no promise to tell Kieren anything. 'Well, thanks for the call, Ricky. See –'

'Jakki! Please don't ring off. There's something else I want to ask about.'

'Well, make it quick, Ricky. You know I've got a sick child to deal with. Lots of extra things to do.'

'Of course, of course. It's just that I wondered if you'd heard anything about Sam – Sam Saxton.'

'Why, is he down with chickenpox, too? Or something worse?' She didn't sound alarmed.

'No, no, not that I know of. I meant, well, generally. You know, what his plans are, that sort of thing.'

'I don't think I could say anything about his plans, Ricky. Sam makes his own decisions, as I'm sure you're aware. Now –'

'So you haven't seen him, then?' Ricky said quickly before the phone could go down at the other end. 'He hasn't involved you in any discussions about the future?'

There was a significant pause before Jakki Kelly replied, 'Ricky, you're obviously desperate to know something. Well, it's not my business to tell you what Sam is thinking but I will tell you this and then you'll know something: Sam will definitely attend Sunday's match against Denholm. I'm sure a lot of people will be pleased to see him, especially when they know one of the things he's got in mind. And that's as far as I can go. Thanks for ringing about Kieren. Give my best to Melanie and Alex. Night, Ricky.'

Very slowly Ricky Todd replaced the phone and began the long process of trying to guess

why Sam Saxton had chosen the Avengers
match as the moment to return to watch his
old team in action.

8 New Leadership

Danny Loxham pushed open the changing-room door, strode into the centre of the room and then suddenly halted as if he'd hit a brick wall. Then slowly he turned through 360 degrees, looking at everything with a sense of wonderment.

'Can't believe this, you know, really can't *believe* it,' he murmured to Alex Todd, who'd followed him in. 'I mean, *I'm* in charge! Never thought it would happen. Captain of the Kings – that's me.'

'Don't forget you've me to thank for it,' Alex told him a little sourly. 'When Dad decided it wouldn't be fair to give the job to me I said you're our best player – after me.'

'Well, I'm going to celebrate,' declared Danny, pushing his hands through his fair hair, one of his ways of expressing confidence. He wasn't making any response to

Alex's claim because he doubted it was true. 'I'm not letting in a single goal this morning. Those Avengers aren't going to put one past me however hard they try. And if I keep a clean sheet for the rest of the season the coach'll have to pick me as skipper for ever!'

'Listen, it won't be all down to you, will it?' Alex pointed out. 'With all these guys out with chickenpox we've got a makeshift defence. So anything could happen if anyone panics or doesn't know what he's doing. That's what Dad says.'

'Hey, I'm not going to be panicking, no way,' announced Josh, overhearing Alex's final words as he came in. 'The coach says I'm improving with every match. Oh, and he thinks I'll strike up a good understanding with Tree and Oats. We'll be really solid at the back, I'm telling you.'

'Make sure you are then. And make *doubly* sure you get the ball up to the strikers so that we can tear Denholm to shreds. They'll never know what's hit 'em when Davey and I get going.'

The boasting and the promises came to an abrupt end a few moments later when Ricky

Todd arrived. Although the coach was dressed in a new purple and white track suit with the words 'Kings Rule!' emblazoned across the chest he appeared to Danny, whose grey eyes rarely missed anything of importance, to be nervous. As if to confirm that suspicion on Danny's part, he even managed to trip over a discarded shoe. Almost petulantly, he kicked it sideways under a bench.

'OK, let's have your attention,' he called in routine fashion even though all the team were looking at him and expecting a pep talk. Then, uncharacteristically, he cleared his throat. 'I don't have to tell you that this is an important match, a *very* important game. Denholm are no mugs. They're higher in the League than us but I'm sure we can beat them in spite of all our problems.'

Josh blinked. Problems? Since when did Ricky Todd admit to anyone that his team had problems? It was the coach's style to exude confidence at all times. Until recently he'd not had much confidence in Josh's abilities but lately he'd changed his mind about that. Yet now he was expressing worries.

'We talked after training about our new defence, our *untried* defence,' he resumed. 'I know Denholm will try to exploit any weaknesses they can find. Seems to me that there are no secrets in this League. Teams seem to know everything they want to know about the opposition and Denholm won't be an exception. But I think we have a new trick that should beat 'em. Our offside trap. This is the time to make the most of it when it's never been seen before. So Josh – and Matthew – and Frazer – keep your concentration, be *aware* of each other. And stay cool. OK?'

He looked in turn at Josh and Matthew Forrest and Frazer McKinnon and received a nod of understanding from each. Ricky had thought of adding that Danny, the new captain, would be right behind them – literally as well as metaphorically – but he didn't want to risk unnerving them with too many words. After all, he would be on the touchline to top up his instructions if necessary.

Alex, impatient with all this talk about the defence, had begun to bounce a ball off the floor as he sat, hunched over, on the bench seat and the rhythm began to build up.

'Alex, stop that!' his father snapped. 'It's very irritating. And you can't be listening if you're making that noise.'

'Sorry, Da – er, Boss,' Alex apologized as he turned pink. His dad had never spoken to him like that before in front of his team-mates.

'OK, well, there's not much more to say except to wish you luck,' the coach added. 'Just remember this: if we get the points today we'll start our climb-back, we'll get to where we belong in this League, up near the top.'

Danny thought that was a rather optimistic view of what they could achieve this season but he wouldn't have dreamed of saying so in front of the coach, especially after Mr Todd had awarded him the honour of the captaincy, albeit on a temporary basis until Joe returned to the team, free of chickenpox. Danny, however, was determined to make the most of the role in the hope that somehow he could retain the armband for the rest of the season. After all, if Joe were to take a long time to recover he might lose his football form altogether.

'How're you feeling, Oats?' he enquired of the well-built Scot who had been drafted into the back line.

'Oh, a wee bit nervous, maybe,' Frazer replied. But his grin suggested he wasn't going to let it really worry him. 'Actually, I quite like playing when it's raining, when the ground is wet. The ball doesn't bounce so high so it's not so, oh, unpredictable, I suppose.'

Danny smiled. 'Good thinking, Oats. But a greasy ball makes things harder for a goalie, you know. Still, if you guys play well I won't be thinking about that, will I?'

Josh, who'd been listening, was reflecting that the rain might have been disastrous for him if he'd been playing in glasses. Fortunately, the weather so far hadn't caused him any difficulties since he'd taken to wearing contact lenses.

The players were on their way out of the changing-room, Ricky's good wishes ringing in their ears, when he remembered something else and told them to wait. 'I meant to tell you that Sam – yes, your old coach – well, he's promised to be here today to see how you're getting on. That's good news because we all want to see him fully fit again, right?'

They chorused their agreement as Ricky hesitated fractionally before adding, 'Be as friendly with him as you like, boys, but remember I'm the one running the team now. So the only instructions that matter are the ones that come from me.'

The Avengers were already on the pitch, immersed in some fast-moving exercises that involved exchanges of passes, first with one foot, then the other. It was the sort of skill-building technique that Ricky had introduced among the Kings and so it had his full approval. At the same time, it made him wonder just how good the Avengers might be. They were in their usual strip of pale blue shirts and shorts, and it occurred to him that it was quite a neat outfit.

Nobody could doubt that Danny was going to enjoy being captain of Rodale Kings JFC. As he marched down the pitch to the centre circle for the traditional pre-game ceremonies involving the officials and the rival skipper his face was wreathed in smiles and he couldn't resist adjusting his captain's armband so that it should be visible to every-one. Then, after winning the toss, which he considered an excellent omen, he chose to play towards the pavilion end, as everyone called it. The pavilion was actually the cricket clubhouse, located on the other side of a boundary path that divided the two sports fields. For some reason no one could explain the Kings always preferred to play that way first.

'Oats, have a good game!' Danny called out loudly, slapping his team-mate on the back as he ran to take up his own position in goal. 'Remember, we're all on your side.'

On the touchline Mrs McKinnon, Frazer's mum, turned to the woman standing beside her. 'Why on *earth* should they call him Oats?' she asked, looking thoroughly bewildered.

'Well, they seem to like nicknames, al-though they don't all have one,' replied Jakki Kelly. 'Marc Thrale is Foggy, for obvious reasons if you hear him shout, and Joe Parbold is Rocky because he's supposed to be the rock on which the defence is built. Oh yes, and Dominic Allenby is sometimes called Domino. Bit obvious, that, but Kieren says that Dominic fell once and brought down two other players at the same time. Somebody said that was the domino effect! Quite clever, really.'

Jakki grinned and seemed to have finished her explanation until Mrs McKinnon prompted her, 'I see, yes, but, well, *Oats*?'

'Oh, sorry. Well, Frazer is Scottish, isn't he, and the boys seem to think all Scots eat porridge. Hence – Oats!'

Sallie McKinnon's vivid blue eyes lit up. 'Oh yes, I *do* see. Well, it makes a change from Jock and Scottie, the usual names awarded by the English. Your son's escaped the labelling process, has he? I'm sorry he's not able to play today, although I suspect his bad luck is Frazer's good luck. How is he?'

'Sitting and suffering, I expect. I mean, he's got over the worst of his chickenpox but he's not allowed to go out yet. Can't have any more players catching it. Probably he and his dad are slumped in front of some rubbish on TV to take their minds off the Kings. Oh, you asked about Kieren's nickname. Nothing so distinctive as the others but they seem to like his initials so he usually just gets KK, or OK for a bit of variety.'

At that moment Frazer thoroughly distinguished himself with a sliding tackle that halted the Avengers' first serious attack of the match. As he picked himself up to shouted applause from his co-defenders Frazer couldn't help glancing towards the touchline. And he was in favour there, too, as his mother clapped enthusiastically.

'Well, I can see Kieren will have a fight on his hands to get back into the team if Frazer carries on like that,' Jakki remarked.

'He practises non-stop, you know,' Sallie disclosed. Jakki knew nothing of the sort but was listening. 'Mostly against his sister, Andrea. Covered in bruises, she's been, all down her legs – but she just loves football, too. Shouldn't be surprised if she doesn't get into a team herself one of these days. She gives as good as she gets, you see.'

The way they were playing at present, there wouldn't be any vacancies in the Denholm ranks. Already the Kings' goal was under siege and twice they'd been forced to concede corners after Danny shouted to his defenders to 'play it safe! Kick it out!' In spite of their unfamiliarity with the formation, the back-line players were combining well, with Josh in outstanding form. It was he who cleared the two most threatening assaults with strong headers and then fearlessly dived into the heart of a hacking scrimmage on the edge of the box to emerge with the ball at his feet and ready to feed Foggy or Lloyd.

Only the attack was failing to function, and that was simply because they weren't getting the ball. On a couple of occasions Davey Stroud drifted back to try to form a link with the defence but Ricky waved him forward again.

'We won't score goals if we don't have players up front, *attacking*,' he'd told them often enough in the hope that the message would be engraved on their minds. Alex never forgot it but Davey was inclined to become impatient if he went too long without a touch of the ball.

Foggy was the weakness, hardly able to control the ball when it came his way and unable to make a telling pass. He appeared so listless that Ricky concluded the normally energetic midfielder was sickening for something. Chickenpox, probably. But the Kings' subs were untried and it could be a fatal decision to replace Foggy so soon.

Then, completely against the run of play, the Kings took the lead.

Lloyd, out on the right, displayed boundless determination to win the ball in a tussle with an opponent who then foolishly jumped feet first at Lloyd in an attempt to wrest the ball back. Jane Allenby started her dash on to the pitch even before the ref signalled that medical services were required for the prostrate Kings' midfielder. And while she ministered to his bruises and scratched shin the ref showed the defender the yellow card.

Ricky managed to attract Matthew Forrest's attention during the hold-up and signalled his requirements by holding both arms high above his head. That, Matthew knew, meant that he was to hit the free kick as hard as possible to send the ball across to the far post. In training, the Kings had been told exactly what to do if Matthew's aim and strength achieved a perfect blend.

When the ball came over it couldn't have

been better placed for Frazer to leap and then head it sideways in the hope that a team-mate would turn it into the net. None of the Kings expected Josh to get there first but the long-legged, fair-haired defender simply hurled himself headlong at the ball to divert it just inside the post from practically a horizontal position.

If everyone else around him was astonished by the swiftness and courage of that strike, Josh himself was ecstatic. It was exactly the sort of goal he'd dreamed about and the success was all the sweeter because officially he was now supposed to be a centre-back.

'Oh, brilliant, Josh, brilliant!' Ricky sang out, hands high above his head again but now to applaud instead of send out signals.

He turned to share the joyousness of the occasion with Jane and at that moment caught sight of Sam Saxton, now standing further along the touchline and also clapping vigorously. So, plainly, he, too, had seen the goal, the culmination of Ricky's tactical planning as well as Josh's daring.

'Great ball, Oats,' Josh told the provider

when he'd disentangled himself from all the celebrations on the pitch. 'Ricky's bound to have seen what you did so I'll bet you're definitely in the team from now on!'

In saying that Josh forgot to think about his own role with the Kings; but then, he sensed he'd already made a good impression on the coach. That happy state didn't alter for him, either, when he caught a glimpse of his old coach, as Josh thought of him. In any case Sam, too, had obviously enjoyed the goal and was nodding approvingly in Josh's direction.

Most of the players were now aware of Sam's presence and Alex was the one who worried about it most. Already disappointed at not being the one to put the ball in the net (he was half a metre away from the ball when Josh dived in), Alex feared that Sam's return might signal the end of his dad's reign as coach. Although he hadn't been nearly as helpful as Alex wanted him to be – especially over the stupid decision to make a *goalkeeper* the captain – his dad would ensure that Alex was never dropped or subbed when he was in goal-scoring vein. But with Sam – well, Sam was capable of causing Alex endless trouble. Moreover, if he came back as coach he'd want to change the system back to the one he himself favoured and probably, out of a spirit of revenge against Ricky for taking his job, he'd drop Alex without a second thought.

Alex was so absorbed by these thoughts that from the kick-off he missed the ball completely when Davey, gaining possession, flicked it on to him. Davey scowled and Alex shot a guilty glance at his dad. Ricky, however, was still experiencing the euphoria of Josh's goal and seemed not to have noticed Alex's carelessness. In any case, Denholm failed to capitalize on the error and within moments were defending again when Lloyd, unaffected by his earlier fall, swept upfield and this time picked out Davey for the final pass.

Davey pulled it down very competently, swivelled, set off at a sharp pace – and was promptly brought down by a sliding tackle from behind. The tackle was made with a very professional edge to it but that didn't prevent it from being illegal. Once again, the Avengers had conceded a free kick at a dangerous distance from their goalmouth. Once again Tree Forrest trotted forward, looked for instructions from Ricky, saw none, and decided to vary his delivery by hitting it low to the near post. Once again, most of the Kings' defence came forward to help out.

And once again, Josh scored.

This time the ball ricocheted from a Denholm ankle on to a Rodale knee and when Alex made a stab at it he merely toe-ended it into Josh's path; and Josh just knew he wasn't going to miss when he lashed out with his left foot. The ball soared into the roof of the net with the goalkeeper completely unsighted.

Josh leapt high enough to win some sort of award for vertical human flight – or so Jane remarked as she shared his second sublime experience within two minutes.

'Who says lightning doesn't strike the same place twice!' she exclaimed to a neighbour.

'Can scarcely believe it!' Ricky murmured, saying precisely what was in his mind. 'I mean, he's been playing well enough in defence but this – well, this is the stuff of schoolboy dreams, isn't it?'

The coach took a quick look along the line of wildly applauding Kings' supporters to see how Sam was reacting this time. Ricky was remembering that Josh told him more than once how Sam had shown no faith in his abilities at all and probably would never have played him in the team again. Thankfully, Ricky didn't have to admit to anyone that he, too, had had doubts about how Josh would really cope at this level whether playing as an attacker or defender. Somehow, though, Josh had overcome his lack of confidence, worked at his game, trained diligently and shown that he could be brave when bravery was needed. So he thoroughly deserved his success. The Kings could be proud of him.

Inevitably, Denholm were eager to strike back immediately. Light blue-shirted attackers swarmed forward, the ball was swept from one wing almost all the way across to the other, and Denholm fans were roaring for a goal. But the breakthrough didn't come. With splendid timing, Rodale's back line moved up in unison just before the ball could be switched to Denholm's leading striker. Thus, when the ball was sent curving into the penalty area, that striker was immediately ruled offside. None of the Rodale defenders had pleaded for the decision and Frazer's was the only arm that had started to go up in appeal.

The referee duly signalled to his assistant that the offside had been noted and the Kings got their anticipated free kick.

'Well judged!' Ricky called to his defenders, adding just one rider. 'Remember, Frazer, don't raise the arm. OK?'

The boy from Scotland nodded his understanding but didn't seem too pleased to be singled out for criticism.

'So what was wrong out there, Ricky?' Jane wanted to know. 'Seemed to me that bit of collective thinking was rather good.'

The coach nodded. 'It was. Just proves that sometimes they really do listen during training! At this level you don't get too much sensible thinking about the offside rule. But it can be a very useful weapon for an organized defence. Today we've got a new formation and so, really, it's much easier to get them to work together on something like this. There's nothing to unlearn, if you like.

The Avengers were looking dangerous there but we, well, outwitted them.'

'Right, but what was Frazer's fault?' Jane was learning all the time about coaching techniques and tactical thinking and she didn't want to miss a trick.

'I don't think it helps at all if players try to influence the ref by raising their arm when they think they've played somebody offside. I'm sure the refs don't take any notice, or if they do, they shouldn't. They've got to make up their own minds,' Ricky explained. 'Also, players themselves are distracted if they're all looking round to see if the ref's going to decide in their favour. Best just to get on with the play, make sure you watch the opposition, not the ref. Our defence today is doing everything just right but Frazer wasn't quite on the ball. He very nearly put his hand up!'

Jane smiled. 'Well, I must say they all looked very professional.'

'Exactly!' the coach beamed. 'Just what I want from them.'

What he got next from his team was another unexpected goal. After being almost completely subdued in the match so far, Foggy suddenly woke up when he intercepted a weak clearance just inside the Denholm half. He appeared hardly to look at what he was doing but his pass to Lloyd couldn't have been better; and Lloyd, seemingly gaining confidence with every passing minute, took two opponents on with wizardry that sent him clear to the by-line. Even there he wasn't finished, nutmegging a challenger before sliding the ball across to Davey. Naturally Alex called for a pass but didn't get one. Davey tenaciously regained possession after a scuffle with a bruising defender and this time decided he was perfectly placed to score.

His shot was well struck and flying towards the bottom of the net when the keeper, flinging himself sideways, got a hand to it and diverted it against the base of his right-hand post. From there the ball rebounded beyond Alex's reach but into the path of Lloyd. With aplomb, Lloyd steered it unstoppably into the opposite corner of the net.

The goalkeeper was Gary Fixby, son of Denholm's former coach and one of the most accomplished in the League. As he got to his knees he couldn't prevent himself pounding the turf with both fists to express his frustration. 'Why does everything have to go wrong for me today – today of *all* days?' he demanded loudly, staring at where he thought heaven or hell must be.

Alex hadn't rushed away to join in the celebrations so he heard what was said. Intrigued, he asked his opponent, 'What're you talking about? What's so special about today?'

Gary stared at him in amazement. 'You really don't know?'

'Just said so, didn't I?' Alex replied sullenly. 'What're you going on about?'

'We're being watched by the guy who's going to choose the next county team, that's all,' Gary revealed. 'Your goalie and I must be the best two in the League, no doubt about that. If he does better than me today then I've had it. And all the bad luck is going *my* way!'

The ref was already gesturing impatiently for Alex to hurry up and take his place in the line-up for the restart. But there was something Alex needed to know first.

'Which guy is it, the one who's picking the team?'

Gary shrugged. 'No idea. Haven't met him – yet.'

When, a couple of minutes later, the whistle went for half-time Alex dashed across to his dad. 'Did you know there's someone here to pick players for the county team?' he demanded even though at that moment Ricky Todd was in the midst of a discussion with Jane about tactics.

'No, I didn't,' was the surprised reply. 'Who is it?'

'Haven't a clue, but I hope he's got his eye on me. Getting into that team could be the first step to getting right to the top.' Alex was already imagining himself as the outstanding captain of a representative side that would deeply impress club managers on the look-out for tomorrow's star players. 'Dad, you've got to find him and tell him I'm playing out of position today and normally score every game. Tell him –'

'But you're *not* playing out of position, Alex.'

'Well, e doesn't know that. And anyway

I'm having to move around a lot because I'm not getting the service a top striker should. That's why other people are fluking our goals. Just tell him, Dad.'

However, Ricky was no longer listening because supporters and other parents had drifted up to offer congratulations on the Kings' outstanding first half. He was also trying to decide whether it would be a good idea to go across and say a welcoming word to Sam Saxton. The former coach also had a circle of admirers and well-wishers and Ricky was concluding it might be diplomatic to say something to him, even though he also believed Sam should have taken the initiative and come to him. On top of all that, he needed to say a few words to his players to ensure they didn't relax against the Avengers. Three goals ought to be sufficient for victory; but Ricky wanted his team to demonstrate to everyone present, and especially to Sam, that they were becoming a brilliant side, just as good in defence as in attack.

Josh, the coach discovered when he at last gathered his players together, was still on a high of highs, almost as if he'd been told he could have a birthday every week of the year. 'So what did you think of my goals, Boss, *really* think of them?' he asked excitedly.

'Great, Josh, just great. From now on you'll have to go up for every free kick, every set piece, every corner. You're doing *exactly* what I want you to do. Just keep it up.'

'Yeah, but don't you want to pick me as a striker from now on?' Josh asked, the intensity of his grin fading a little.

'Look, you're having a terrific match, Josh. Just make that centre-back position your own. I need top players in every position in the team, OK?'

'Hear, hear!' exclaimed Serena Colmer, whose delight at the way things were going was at least as great as Josh's. 'Lloyd's really buzzing, isn't he? Never known him so thrilled. You're doing a great job, Ricky.'

Lloyd didn't look the slightest bit embarrassed by those remarks as probably he would have done on another occasion. By now he and his team-mates knew of the presence of the selector and were discussing who might attract his interest. The way Denholm were playing, it was obvious he wouldn't be much interested in them.

Danny identified a problem. 'It's all right for you lot, you're turning it on and he can see that. But I've had nothing to do yet. He hasn't had a chance to see how good I am! That's not right, is it?'

Alex, however, wasn't sympathetic. 'Let's keep it that way,' he grinned. 'We need the ball badly down the other end so I can score a hat-trick!'

By the start of the second half it seemed that everyone knew that a county selector was present and jotting down likely names in his notebook. Play slowed down as attackers and defenders alike began to dwell on the ball, attempting elaborate feats of control, dribbling and possession. As soon as someone parted with the ball he usually called for its return. When anyone was within sight of goal, spectacular shots were fired off. But, as they managed easily to save all of them, Danny Loxham and Gary Fixby were pleased enough about that, especially Danny, who was eager to practise his new skill in distribution, the long over-arm throw to a team-mate.

'Come on, Kings, we haven't won yet – let's attack 'em!' Ricky yelled in frustration at what was going on. It seemed to him that the Avengers were getting more into the game and sensed that if they got one goal back they might well scent at least a draw or even a win. Sam, he saw, was now on his own, Jakki Kelly having disappeared on some errand or other. She might even, it occurred to him, have returned home to see how Kieren was getting on. Ricky bit his lip in annoyance as he remembered he hadn't taken the trouble to ask how the boy was feeling today (and he should also have enquired when his dedicated defender might be fit enough to play again).

'Oh, great tackle, Oats, good stuff!' Danny called encouragingly as he swooped to pick up the ball when it ran loose as a result of Frazer's interception. Not for a single moment had Danny forgotten that he was now the captain of the Kings. When he'd hurled the ball back to Frazer just outside the box now he made the point of adjusting the armband in a rather theatrical fashion just in case his old coach hadn't noticed the badge of promotion. Sam, though, seemed to be studying a sheet of paper he'd taken from an inside pocket.

'Well played, Frazer, keep it up!' Ricky applauded. It was now clear to the coach that Frazer had improved immensely since he'd first taken part in a five-a-side game. His ability certainly hadn't been evident then but the boy had listened intelligently to all he'd been told in training and now was proving his adaptability. So far he hadn't put a foot wrong. Ricky was entitled to congratulate himself on his own judgement. Without doubt, Frazer McKinnon could be regarded as the Kings' find of the season.

Soon, though, pale blue shirts were no longer to be seen in numbers around the Kings' penalty area. The Avengers were losing their bite as time ran out and it was clear they weren't going to win this match and thus hold on to their superior position in the League. Increasingly, play was switching to the other end. Alex was calling for the ball again, *demanding* it from any team-mate in possession. 'I've got to score, *got* to,' he urged himself on. But it wasn't to be his day. When the fourth and final goal arrived it was his rival striker, Davey Stroud, who put the ball in the net without any contribution at all from Alex in the build-up.

Tree Forrest, apparently gaining confidence by the minute, broke away down the right after collecting another throw from Danny. Instead of hoofing a pass to Lloyd or Foggy he simply kept going, his energy seemingly inexhaustible. Denholm's depressed mid-fielders appeared to give up the chase when Tree swept past them. He was enjoying himself far too much to answer pleas for a pass from Alex and Davey. His run ended only when he stumbled over a large divot and then went down under a delayed challenge from an opponent. It wasn't a foul by any stand-ards but the ref, who had shown excellent judgement until then, awarded a free kick a couple of metres to the right of the box.

Indicating very firmly that he intended to take the kick himself, Tree calmly dusted himself down, assuring everyone that he'd come to no harm in the fall. That minor delay allowed Josh to steal across to the opposite side of the area; and from that position he hoped to run in, leap and head the ball firmly past Denholm's out-of-luck keeper. All that went wrong with his plan was that Tree hit the ball with his usual power directly to where Josh had stationed himself. So all Josh could do was to out-jump his nearest opponent and head the ball down for Alex to try a shot on the half-volley. It was struck fiercely and almost on target; but the ball flashed back off the inside of the post with Gary Fixby left helpless. By good fortune Davey was perfectly placed to stun the ball with one foot and then slot it into the net with the other. Rodale Goal Kings 4 Denholm Avengers 0.

Once again, Alex was left in total despair. Nothing in the world, he believed, was going right for him. Unless . . . unless . . . the county selector had seen that the player who really deserved to be credited with that goal was the slim, wavy-haired, two-footed striker with the number nine on his shirt: Alex Todd. Surely *everyone* present without defective eyesight must have seen that?

Ricky glowed. Applauding with hands high above his head, he was sure now his luck had turned. The team were playing their best football for weeks, following instructions to the letter and it must be obvious to all that he was doing a marvellous job. So he couldn't help glancing towards Sam. And that was the moment Sam chose to come across for a word.

'Good performance,' he said, holding out his hand to Ricky and then to Jane as if he knew she was now a member of the Kings' coaching staff. 'You've done a good job, Ricky, getting them to play as well as this. Must say, Josh has surprised me. Got a real eye for a goal now, hasn't he?'

Ricky nodded. He really hadn't expected such praise from his predecessor. So he smiled and simply murmured, 'Well, everything seems to be working. I think Josh recognizes now that he can be a good defender and still get vital goals for us.'

'Sam, you did the same, you know – you turned Dominic into a top defender,' Jane reminded him. 'You gave him a real purpose in the game and he's enjoying every minute of it.'

Sam raised his hand to his baseball cap in a familiar gesture. 'Kind of you to remember that, Jane. Tapping into a player's true abilities is what coaching is all about, I suppose.' He turned back towards Ricky. 'I'm impressed by your off-side plan as well as the whole defensive set-up. Maybe you should hire another bus to celebrate more success! That plainly brings good results.'

Ricky couldn't tell whether Sam was being sarcastic or not, so he had to give him the benefit of the doubt. After all, Sam didn't have to come over to make complimentary remarks, a wave and a raised thumb would have been perfectly acceptable.

'Sometimes everyone needs a boost and I think that's what we got with the bus,' Ricky grinned. 'So, sure, we may try it again one day. Anyway, Sam, how're things with you? Are you missing the game? Feeling left out of things?'

'Oh, I'm not out of the game. I'm very much back in it. Didn't you know?'

Ricky's heart missed a beat. Was Sam about to announce that he was planning to take over the Kings again? If so . . .

'Yes, I'm getting a new team together and I'm hoping some of these boys will be playing for us,' Sam was continuing after the briefest of pauses. 'I imagined you'd heard. News and rumours always travel fast in football circles in my experience.'

'Well, er, nothing definite,' Ricky responded, trusting that he didn't sound totally ignorant of whatever was going on in Sam's world.

'I've been asked to select a representative squad for a game against London schools. Quite an honour, really. For me, as well as for the boys I choose, I mean.' Sam watched with interest as worry lines on Ricky's face began to fade. 'Seems that a lot of people don't want me to go out of the game so this is a way for me to get my hand in again. May lead to other things as well. But I'm really looking forward to working with players I've already coached. And, of course, new ones.'

'Oh –' began Ricky, still wondering what to say, when the final blast of the ref's whistle brought the game to an end and saved the Kings' coach from having to make any comment at all for the moment.

Together the two men vigorously clapped the players from the pitch and it was noticeable that practically every one of the Kings tried to catch Sam's eye; and most of them succeeded.

'Really good game, that,' enthused Sam. 'On that sort of form, the Kings should soon be bounding up the League table. You've got plenty to be optimistic about there, Ricky.'

'Thanks. But it, er, sounds as if you've got plenty to look forward to, Sam.'

'Definitely! You'll be hearing from me soon and so will some of our boys. No doubt about that at all.'

If you particularly enjoy reading about football, why not try some of these other Faber children's books?

Goal Kings by Michael Hardcastle

BOOK ONE: Shoot-Out
BOOK TWO: Eye for a Goal
BOOK THREE: And Davey Must Score
BOOK FOUR: They All Count

Life in the Junior Football League can be tough. This adventure-packed series follows the dramas and excitements – on and off the pitch – in the lives of Goal Kings JFC.

Own Goal by Michael Hardcastle

Russell is passionate about football but he has a problem: he scores own goals. Then, amazingly, he discovers a footballing talent he never dared dream of.

One Kick by Michael Hardcastle

Jamie finds that all is not fair play on the

field, and makes a mistake that is to haunt him for weeks and almost put a stop to his footballing career . . .

Second Chance by Michael Hardcastle

Scott is an ace striker. But when he moves to a school where soccer comes a poor second to cricket, he faces an unexpected and difficult challenge . . .

Frances Fairweather: Demon Striker!
by Derek Smith

Frances is so obsessed with football that she gets thrown out of the girls' team, and the boys' team won't have her either. Drastic measures are called for: Frances decides to become 'Frank' . . .

Faber children's books are available from bookshops. For a complete catalogue, please write to: The Children's Marketing Department, Faber and Faber, 3 Queen Square, London WC1N 3AU.